FURTHER ADVENTURES OF JAMES JOYCE

ALSO BY COLM HERRON

For I Have Sinned

FURTHER ADVENTURES OF JAMES JOYCE

Colm Herron

Published in 2010 by Dakota

ISBN 978 0 954645 31 1

Printed and bound in the UK by
CPI Mackays, Chatham ME5 8TD

To the real Myles Corrigan without whom this novel would never have been completed.

Myles Corrigan wasn't in good shape. Sodden and sullen, ratty and reckless, and with the hangover already biting, he emerged from The Drunken Dog into the arms of two Royal Greenjackets.

- Author! Author!

- Thanks very much but I've only just started. Your acclaim should come at the end.

- Acclaim? I'm not acclaiming you. I'm pulling you up. What's all this about sodden? You're implying drink-sodden, aren't you?

- Yes.

- Then why don't you write what you mean?

- I thought sodden went better with sullen.

- It may go better but it's not true. Writers are supposed to tell the truth.

- Are they? Do they?

- Yes. Don't they? Anyway, none of the two of them's true. I was not drink-sodden. I had a little too much to drink but I was NOT drink-sodden. I was nauseous.

- Okay. How about "sick and sullen, ratty and reckless, and with the hangover—"

- Right. That's okay. The rest will do. Proceed. With care.

already biting, he emerged from The Drunken Dog into the arms of two Royal Greenjackets.

He sorely regretted having spent so much of the evening in the company of John Jameson & Son. Late on, noisy bonhomie had given way to serious differences of opinion culminating in the older Jameson thrusting a large kitchen knife into the centre of Myles' forehead just below the hairline and Jameson *fils* forcing the blade further into the skull in the manner of a battering ram so that the point finally exited at the back, almost certainly carrying some brain matter with it.

- Roight, said Soldier A. - Stop where you are, mate.

- Yeah, what is it this time? responded Myles.

- Wot's that? said Soldier B.

I wasn't talking to you. Slimy limey.

- What was it you wanted to see me about? said Myles with as much restraint as he could muster.

- Come again? said Soldier A.

An invitation I won't be extending to you, Britprick. God but you're ugly.

- You having us on? asked Soldier B.

- Look, said Myles. - I've just finished six hours in that place behind me and I'm in no mood for jokin.

- You work there? asked Soldier B.

- Work! It's much more serious than that. I drink there.

- We've got a roight one here, said Soldier A.

- Okay, mate. Name? said Soldier B.

8

- You want my name?

- Yeah. Name.

- James Augustine Joyce.

- Very impressive, said Soldier A. - That's Roman, isn't it?

- Cork, actually, said Myles. - Though I have heard it said—

- Address?

- The Martello Tower....

- Martello Tower.

- ...but I'm not goin back.

- Why's that then?

- Two people tried to kill me there last night.

- Really? How was that? Did you report it?

- They both had drink taken, explained Myles. - But I want to make it clear right now that Samuel Trench shot at me in good faith. *He* took me for a panther. The other, however—

- Wot was his name again? The first one.

- Trench. Samuel Trench.

- Trench. Roight. And who was the other party?

- The other bastard was Oliver Saint John Gogarty. Wants to be a doctor. Trainin to save lives. I ask you. A dirty little traitor. He wanted me out of the tower and he didn't care how he did it. He only pretended to have delirium tremens.

- Wot? Wot's that?

- The DTs.

- I see. Where is this tower?

- Sandycove.

- Where's that?

9

- It's near Bray. In County Wicklow.

- Never heard of it.

- Really? It's actually not much more than an ass's roar from Dublin.

- Dublin. Wot's brought you to Londonderry then?

- Ah. That's another story. I suppose you could say I was moved by the spirit.

- Spirit?

- Well, spirits. John Jameson and Sons to be precise.

- **Stop. It's not Sons. It's Son.**

- **Sons.**

- **Son. You wrote Son earlier on.**

- **I was wrong. It's Sons.**

- **It's John Jameson and SON. Do you not think I've seen that label enough times to know?**

- **It's John Jameson and Sons plural.**

*My God. Maybe he's right. I **thought** there was another one. That shifty-looking character with the drill that kept giving me dirty looks as if I owed him money or something. Yes, I can see him now, leaning over me just as I nodded off. Looked like a drunken dentist. And as dour as fuck, if I remember right.*

- HQ have no record of your name, said Soldier B. - I have to ask you for your date of birth.

- Certainly, responded Myles. - The second of the second eighty-two.

- The wot?

The door of The Drunken Dog opened and a tall greyhaired man came out.

- The second of the second eighty-two.

- That, sir, would make you six years old. I have to warn you.

- What do you mean, six years old! I was born on the second of February, eighteen eighty-two. Groundhog Day. Did you know that?

Conn Doherty stood frowning, one foot on the pub step, the other on the pavement. After a few moments he moved forward to join the company.

- Excuse me, he said. - If you don't mind. Could I just explain—

- Who are you? demanded Soldier A.

- Conn Doherty. This is a friend of mine, Myles Corrigan.

- Wot name did you say? said Soldier B.

- Conn Doherty.

- No. His name.

- Myles Corrigan. And don't listen to him about his date of birth. He was born in nineteen thirty-nine.

- He's just given us false information then, said Soldier A.

- Jack, phone for a landrover.

- What do you want a landrover for? asked Conn.

- To take him in for questioning, said Soldier A. - Okay Jack.

- Please, said Conn. - He won't remember any of this in the mornin. He's not fit to be questioned.

- Who's not fit? snapped Myles. - WHO's not fit? I'm fit for questionin and I'm fit for answerin. Listen to this: O dear me. Poor Molly Milligan, humdrumming on her sewing machine of a soulboring summer noon, searsunlight fallfallfalling on Derry's pavesplit pathaways.

- You have to understand, pleaded Conn. - He does this sometimes. Did he tell you his name was James Joyce?

- Yes, he did, answered Soldier A. - James Augustine Joyce.

- Hang on, said Soldier B. - I know now. Isn't he the writer?

- That's right, said Conn. - This man has Joyce on the brain. He's wastin your time. But he's on medication, you see. He shouldn't be drinkin at all.

- He did porn, didn't he? said Soldier B. - He had to leave the country. Roight?

- What! snapped Myles. - How dare you! Hah! Who do you think you are? Not even the papal nuncio would say that. Not anymore. Who sent you? Tell me, who sent you?

- Look, let him go, said Conn. - I'll put him in a taxi.

- You telling us wot to do? said Soldier A.

- Oh no, said Conn.

- It sounds loike that to me, said Soldier A.

- Uh oh, said Myles, putting a hand on Conn's shoulder.

- You know what this is like, don't you? Classic case. It's like when you think somebody's drowndin and you jump in to save him and you end up getting drownded yourself and all the other one was doin was messin about with a couple of mates in the water.

- Can I have your date of birth, sir? said Soldier A. - You're not obliged to give it but—

- The seventh of September, nineteen forty.

- Did you know, Conn, said Myles, - that when the pope announced he was infallible at the first Vatican Council in eighteen seventy some of the cardinals got up to walk out?

12

Will I tell you what the pope said to them?

- Hold on. Quoiet a minute, said Soldier B. He spoke into his mouthpiece.

- Conn Doherty. Seventh of September, nineteen forty, he intoned.

- He said, "You be damned!" continued Myles. - "Kissmearse! I'm infallible!" Did you know that?

- No, said Conn.

Myles turned to the two Royal Greenjackets.

- Did you gentlemen know that? "Kissmearse". That's what he said. Would you believe it?

- Roight. Will do. Roger and out, said Soldier B. He looked at Myles and Conn.

- You two can go. Hop it.

The Greenjackets turned and walked up the Strand Road, one backwards and one forward.

- No manners, said Myles. - How many times have I told you? Neither breedin nor manners. The sooner they leave this country for good the better. That's the only Roger and out I want to hear.

- There's something wrong here, Colm. Is it all right if I call you Colm, by the way?

- No, it's not all right. Herron is the name. Mister Herron.

- Oh?

- Yes. None of my characters should be on first name terms with me.

- Why's that then?

- I have to stay detached. I have to be in control. What was your question?

13

- It isn't a question. It's an observation.

- Right. Observe away.

- There's something wrong. You accepted back at the start that I wasn't drunk, yet now you have me going on like a naggled newt.

- Naggled? What does that mean?

- I don't know. Well, I do know but —

- I'm not using that. It's not even a word.

- Neither is humdrumming. You said Molly Milligan was humdrumming.

- And so she was. She was empty and bored and restless. Suffering from what the French call *ennui*.

- Very fancy footwork, Monsieur. But you can't get round me that easily. We were talking about my alcohol level.

- Ah yes. Your alcohol level.

- Half an hour ago, if you remember, I was a little over the limit and now suddenly I'm sozzled.

- Not really. You lurch between banter and bloody-mindedness. But that's you. That's the way you are with drink in you, especially when you mix it with your medication.

- Hmmm. It seems to me that it suits your purpose to have me barking out of my back end. Am I right?

- No you're not right. But now that you're on the subject of suiting my purpose, there's something I've been meaning to tell you.

- Oh?

- Yes. I'm not sure how to say this but... I'm seriously

14

thinking of getting rid of you.

- What do you mean, getting rid of me! You can't do that.

- I can't do that? Who's writing this book, you or me? You're a very difficult character, you know.

- You're never going to get it done without me.

- Really?

- Yeah. I'm central. I'm pivotal. Look at my wit. My profound thoughts.

- They're mine. They're all mine. You're nothing but a figment. I can finish you off anytime I want. There's a war going on here you know.

- Hold on. You can't just get rid of me when you're hardly started.

- Hitchcock got rid of Janet Leigh after— how long was it?

- An hour and ten minutes.

- More like half an hour. And it was only when she was dead that the film took off.

- So you'd just write on and forget I ever existed.

- Not at all. People will be remembering you for the rest of the book. They'll never stop talking about how great a bastard you were.

- Listen, can we just forget about this? All I was trying to do was keep you right. Every author needs a collaborator.

- Not this one. You know what happens to collaborators in this part of the world, don't you?

- Now you're just being —

- They get shot.

- You wouldn't!

- I don't know. Look, just leave me alone and let me think.

- Okay. Okay. Sorry I spoke.

- Did you see the nature programme on BBC2 last night? said Brian.

- Nope.

- It was a scream, whispered Brian. - There were these sea creatures in it that seemed to have just the two parts— a brain and a penis.

- Sounds like the average Derry woman's lot to me, said Conn.

- Except she usually doesn't get the brain thrown in, said Brian.

- But you wanted to see them goin after the females. They were like thousands of frenchies flappin in the breeze.

- Flappers after slappers.

- It's like the one about the medical student.

The staff room door opened and two women carrying large handbags walked in.

- We were thinking of goin to the Algarve this year, said Mrs D'Arcy. - I hear it's lovely.

- It depends what month you go, said Mrs Doherty. - In July—

- We were in Egypt last year, said Mrs D'Arcy. - Cairo. I wouldn't go back.

- I remember you sayin, said Mrs Doherty.

- The hotel was brilliant and all. Great food and lovely rooms. Heated pool and everythin. But the poverty was terrible.

- Aw aye.

- The second day we were there we took a walk and we were hardly out of the hotel when these two little boys came over to us beggin—

- Aw aye. It's supposed to be a very poor country.

- and I handed them a bar of chocolate between them. Well, you should have seen it. They went at each other like two savages. The bigger one left the smaller one with a fractured skull.

- My God. You're not serious.

- Over a bar of chocolate. We took him to the hospital and we even waited to see that his parents were contacted. But do you know. He didn't even have a home. No parents. No home.

- O   my   God. That must have been terrible for you.

- It ruined our holiday. The whole thing cost nearly two thousand pounds for me and Kevin and the three children. I couldn't get to sleep that night thinking of the poor boy. That's the worst—

The rest was lost in a tide of incoming voices as the staff room filled quickly and noisily. Conn sat hunched in a corner beside Brian, sipping his tea and listening to the clink and the chatter.

If this meeting doesn't start soon, he thought, it's not going to end soon. Maybe I'll tell them I'm not well and just go. I could take two days off. No, three. More convincing.

- Do you not think so? said Brian.

- Sorry. What were you sayin?

- Naw, I was sayin, teachin's gone to the dogs. Do you remember the days we used to be able to go home at half three?

- Seems like about twenty years ago, said Conn. - How long is it?

- Six weeks, said Brian. - Hey, here come Darby and Joan. Would you look.

Mister McGrotty and Gerry McEldowney came into the staff room together, their shoulders shaking with quiet laughter. They stood chuckling for a little and then Mister McGrotty said - Sorry for keeping you, ladies and gentlemen. Gerry's just been telling me about the Education Guidelines meeting he was at in Belfast yesterday. I'm sure you all appreciate how lucky we are to have a representative on the Guidelines panel.

- Only he's not representative, whispered Brian.

- So we can have this regular blow by blow account of the state of play. Anyway, I'll leave you all in the capable hands of Gerry.

Mister McGrotty moved across the room and stood, arms folded, his back against a window sill.

- I'd just like to thank Mister McGrotty, said Gerry, - for those kind words.

He smiled self-deprecatingly and began to shuffle papers in his hand.

- Well, I'll get straight into it. There was good progress

made at yesterday's meeting in Stormont and you'll be receiving some literature about it in due course. However, when I got back home last night, I typed out a summary of our deliberations and, if you don't mind reading it, it'll give you a bit of insight into the latest thinking on auracy and the primacy of language development.

- Jesus, breathed Conn. - This is a bit hard on the system.

- This *is* the system, whispered Brian.

The typed sheets were passed around. Conn looked at his copy and sighed.

- This doesn't actually mean anything, does it? he asked Brian.

- Of course not, said Brian.

Gerry read out everything that was on the sheets. Conn sat trying to relax his clenched jaw. *Start with the face, then the neck, then the rest of you. Keep the ulcer away.*

- This is an evolutionary process, said Gerry when he'd finished reading aloud. - We haven't come to any definitive conclusions as yet. These observations are meant merely as... as pointers. Guidelines, like it says on the tin.

Mister McGrotty smiled down at his shoes.

- How did he pronounce that? muttered Conn. - Evilutionary. He's an evilutionary.

- Steady on, whispered Brian.

- You mark my words, muttered Conn. - That boy's goin to career to the top.

- Any questions?

Gerry stood looking around, a slight smile on his lips. A slither of ice stopped and started and stopped and started on

19

its way down a window pane and then splashed playfully on the outside sill.

- Well, said Gerry. - That about does it. I've a staff meeting pencilled in for next... Wednesday. Isn't that right, Mister McGrotty?

Mister McGrotty nodded vigorously.

- Wednesday. Yes. All right, everybody?

There were no sounds of dissent.

- You'll be getting a fuller account of our deliberations by the start of next week, said Gerry. - If you'll all just have a look over it before our next get-together.

A head popped up and then down.

- I was just... said Annette Givens. - Sorry.

Gerry looked at her inquiringly and Mister McGrotty said - Yes, Annette?

- If it's all right with everybody, she said, - I... I...

And then it all came out in a rush.

- I'd like to read out a short poem a girl in my class wrote today.

- That's okay, responded Mister McGrotty. - Go right ahead, Annette.

- It's just that it's so, so striking and sensitive. It's actually...by Ciara, your granddaughter, Mister McGrotty. I thought it was just brilliant. I really think it should be published.

There was a suck and a click and a cluck of tongues. Deirdre Watson and Fionnuala McEneaney were stooped, heads together.

- Did you ever have misgivins? whispered Conn.

- Once, many years ago, Brian whispered back. - Sure

that's how I got the bloody hernia.

- I often wondered about that.
- Honest to God, I don't know what came over me.
- Rush of blood to the gusset?
- I think that might have been it.

Annette Givens coughed and began tremulously:

> - So many dead,
>
> So many from both sides.

She coughed again.

> - So much fear, so much hate.
>
> I want to scream
>
> When I think of those who cause it.

The voice was stronger now.

> - Do they not see
>
> They have no right,
>
> No cause worth talking about,
>
> Worth fighting about?
>
> All they're doing
>
> Is destroying, destroying, destroying.
>
> When will they ever learn?
>
> When will it ever end?

She looked around, embarrassed and pleased.

- I thought it was so insightful, she said.
- It certainly is, said Mister McGrotty. - I feel very proud of Ciara.
- It's beautiful, said Mrs McGarvey. - And true.
- All good writing comes from the heart, said Mrs Farren.

There was a shuffling of shoes and Gus Hazlitt leaned forward, half standing.

21

- I would say that that poem is the most remarkable expression of mind and soul I've ever heard from a child, he said.

His hand was in the air, index finger rising and falling as if knocking ash from a cigarette.

- I would even go as far as to say, he continued, - that she was inspired by the Holy Spirit when she wrote it.

He sank slowly back to his seat and then got half up again.

- That was inspiring, Annette, he said.

No one spoke for several moments and then Gerry McEldowney said to Annette - Ciara's come on a lot. When I started taking your class for language development last September she had very little confidence. Do you remember? She actually shied away from expressing herself.

He paused and then said - That's really remarkable.

There was an uncertain gathering up of handbags. It stopped when Mister McGrotty moved away from the window sill and motioned to Gerry to sit down.

- There's just one other thing, he said. His voice was grave but his face was smiling. - I just wanted to tell you all that, after a lot of soul searching, I've come to a decision about my future. I've decided that I'll be retiring at the end of the school year.

The only other sound was a woman's Oh from near the back of the room.

- Forty years is a long sentence to serve, continued Mister McGrotty, - and I hope I've served it well. I have the option, of course, of going on till I'm sixty-five but I've decided that, all things considered, it's time for the full stop.

He turned and gestured towards Mister Donegan.

- I've already told Simon of my decision and he in turn has informed me that he will be retiring at the same time as me.

He lowered his hand.

- So. The two top positions will be there to be filled.

There was silence.

- So. I'll see you all next Wednesday, if not before.

There was more silence and then the handbags were gathered up again.

- Sometimes I think, said Myles, - there must be better ways of spendin the night.

- Than what? asked Conn.

- Than sittin in The Drunken Dog till two in the morning. It's not worthy of me. Sittin with all those refugees. You know, it's like as if it's a sanctuary from the real world. I'm talkin complete shite with some dead-eyed loser at ten to two and I'm sayin to myself, What the fuck am I doin here? I mean, this guy's subnormal. He can hardly string two syllables together and here's me—

- Maybe you're a bit of a refugee yourself, said Conn.

- Naw, said Myles. - What I am is a voluntary exile. Different.

Conn reached out his foot and nudged a smouldering table leg from the footpath onto the straggling barricade that lay outside Pilots' Row Centre. Myles followed him through the narrow gap.

- You could always sit in the flat and read a good book, Conn said.

- I've read all the good books. You tell me one I haven't read.

- *White Thighs?*

- Read it.

- *The Whip Angels?*

- Read it twice.

They rounded the corner of William Street.

- That looks like a fire, said Conn.

- It *is* a fire, said Myles. - What place is it?

- It's Hutton's butchers. Jesus. I think there's people livin in flats there.

Black smoke and little spits of flame were tumbling out of one of the first floor windows. A girl, bare to the waist, had a pyjamad leg out over the other windowsill.

- My God. Look at that, said Conn.

- Yeah, said Myles. - Look at those breasts.

They ran the twenty yards to Hutton's and Conn shouted - Go and tell the soldiers to ring the fire brigade and ambulance.

Myles stumbled over a broken brick, steadied himself and zigzagged among the leftovers from the lunchtime rioting. He turned the bend at Chamberlain Street and saw the soldiers standing at the checkpoint in Waterloo Place, guns at the ready.

- Fire! he shouted.

One soldier emerged from the shadow of a doorway and

raised his rifle to his shoulder.

I don't think they heard me.

- Fire! he shouted, louder.

- Stop! Hold your fire!

The cutglass accent sliced through the semidark.

Christ. That Sandhurst bastard just saved my life.

- Listen to me! he howled. - There's a fire in a flat up around the corner and there's people trapped inside. Phone the fire brigade. Please. And an ambulance.

Conn placed his overcoat around the girl's shoulders and fastened a button. Her eyes glittered gratefully up at him.

- Are you okay? he asked.

- I think so, she answered. She had long red hair and the face of a nymph.

- Is there anybody else in the buildin?

- No. Nobody lives in the top flat. And my boyfriend's away out for the night. I've got the flu.

- Oh God, said Conn.

She huddled against him and put her arm around his stomach.

Fingers and palms on dewy wet skin. Flashing eyes and flaming hair. Fever in her hot little body.

- The firemen are on their way. An ambulance too, he said.

People have gathered. Where do they all come out of? I hear them watching me. They can talk all they want. Nobody can say a word.

- I don't need an ambulance, she said. - I'll go to my mother's.

Suddenly she became very tense.

- My things, she breathed. - Our things. They're in there.

They both looked up. The flames ran over the windowsill like running water. The *der ner* of a fire engine sang from somewhere and the winking blue ambulance was waiting behind them.

- As long as *you're* all right, said Conn.

- Thanks, she said. She clung closer.

- What's your name? he asked.

- Melanie. What's yours?

- Conn. Conn Doherty.

Derry's dark-eyed rescuer of the night. Mysterious. Modest. Kind. Horny as hell.

- Listen to this, said Gus Hazlitt. - Would you call this responsible journalism? 'LETTER BOMBER PRAYS FOR PEACE.'

- That about Shane? asked Pippa.

- Aye. But he's not a letter bomber. He's an ex-letter bomber.

- Imagine, said Pippa. - Twelve years for makin letter bombs out of a school science kit.

- Twelve years so *far*, said Gus. - Listen: 'Shane Paul O'Doherty yesterday made another dramatic appeal for his freedom from Long Kesh prison. The ruthless letter bomber has renounced violence and is now said to spend twelve hours in his cell each day praying for his enemies and for an end to the IRA's murderous campaign against the Protestant people

26

of Ulster.'

- Where did you get that paper?

- I found it lyin in the staff room. Somebody actually paid money for this.

- Can you not get any of them to support you?

- They're not interested. They all know what I'm doin but none of them are interested.

- What about Conn Doherty? He was always friendly with you.

- He blames the British for everythin. He says the IRA are only a symptom. Did you ever hear of a symptom blowin somebody's head off?

- It's terrible, said Pippa. - Sometimes— God forgive me— sometimes I get so upset with the Holy Spirit for not wakenin people up.

- The Spirit only comes if you look for Him, said Gus. - You know that, Pippa.

- But it's so simple. They're teachers. Can they not see?

- You know who's a great man? Father Denis Faul. The way he got those IRA prisoners to reject violence. If he can just get the British to let them out on licence the floodgates will open.

- Please God, said Pippa. She got up from the couch and went over to Gus. - I forgot to ask you, is the bishop comin here or what?

- No. I have to collect him.

- And are you sure youse are goin to get in this time?

- Aye, said Gus. - it's sorted . It's ridiculous when you think about the way a couple of Republican troublemakers actin the maggot can stop thousands of relatives visitin.

- Sometimes I get so discouraged.

- Don't be, said Gus. He looked fondly at her and took her by the hand. - Will we say a prayer before I go?

She smiled and put her arm around his waist.

- Okay, she said.

They knelt together on the carpet and looked up at the picture above the mantelpiece. A large white dove hovered protectively over the earth, its wide open wings rimmed by the rising sun.

- Come O Holy Spirit, they prayed, - enlighten our minds and fill our hearts with Thy love. Send forth Thy Spirit and we shall be created and Thou shalt renew the face of the earth.

Myles folded six beer mats neatly across the middle and placed them upright in a straight line.

- You didn't tell me Ciaran McGrotty was retirin, he said.

- I didn't bother, said Conn. - I didn't think you'd be that interested.

- Are you applyin?

- I am not.

- You should, said Myles. - They couldn't give it to anybody else.

- I don't want it.

- Of course you do.

- Naw I don't, said Conn. - It's the priests. I couldn't stomach bein all cosy with them.

- Listen, it's a business arrangement. You run the school, they run the board. There'd be no conflict.

- You're jokin. Anyway, they'd never appoint me.

- What do you mean? said Myles. - Why wouldn't they?

He touched the beer mat nearest him with his fingertip and all six went down like dominoes.

- Right, said Conn. - Do you want to know my qualifications?

- Shoot.

- Ciaran McGrotty has his knife in me and he's a drinkin partner of Josie Rabbitt the buildin contractor.

- So far so good.

- Josie Rabbitt is now vice-chairman of the board of governors and he can make them do whatever he wants. He's in half the school boards in the town and he's there to keep people like me out.

- I like it!

- Father Babb's the chairman of the board and in nineteen eighty-one I got on to him for sayin that the hungerstrikers in Long Kesh were suicidal maniacs.

- That's right. I remember. You tore into him, didn't you?

- I thought I was pretty mild actually. I just asked him did he not think it was time he stopped spoutin British propaganda.

- Sounds mild enough to me. How'd he take it by the way?

- Great. He clasped me to his bosom and gave me a love heart. How the fuck d'you think he took it!

- Naw, really. What did he say?

- I don't remember exactly, said Conn. - Somethin about me bein a fine example to the children of All Saints.

- You see? You're half way there already.

Myles slipped the folded beer mats into his pocket and shouted

- Hey, Pat, you wouldn't give us a drink there, would you?

Pat came in from the lounge with a tea towel over his shoulder.

- Sure thing, Myles, he said. - Another Jameson?

- Yeah, and a Guinness for Doherty.

- Up and comin, said Pat.

Myles turned to Conn.

- Hey, what do you think of this one? he said. - It just came to me last night when I was goin to sleep. It's called The Prayer for the Protection of Catholic Schools:

> Blessed Michael the Archangel,
> Defend us in the hour of Conflict!
> Be our safeguard against
> The wickedness and snares of the Conn man!
> May God restrain him, we humbly pray,
> And wilt thou, O prince of the heavenly host,
> Thrust Doherty down to hell
> And with him all the other wicked wankers
> Who slurry through our schools
> For the ruination of souls!

Conn laughed.

- Not bad for a lapsed Catholic, he said.

- What do you mean, lapsed Catholic? said Myles. - I'm a diabolical apostate. Sure every time I meet Gus Hazlitt he whips a crucifix from inside his shirt and holds it up to my face.

30

- He's not that bad.

- Naw, but I am. Tell me, is he applyin?

- I can't see it, said Conn. - There's only one thing he wants and that's to convert the world to the Holy Spirit.

Pat left the whiskey on the table.

- Thanks Pat, said Myles. - May you see your children's children.

- Jesus, I hope not, said Pat. - Me own wur bad enough. I couldn't wait to git them outa the house.

- Any word of that Guinness? said Conn.

- Aw, right. I'll put it on now for you, said Pat and went behind the bar.

- You wouldn't need to be dyin of thirst in this place, said Conn to Myles. He took a slow sip of his dregs.

- Who's all applyin? asked Myles. - The usual suspects?

- As far as I know.

- There's somethin I can't understand. How the hell did a boy like McGrotty ever get to be headmaster in the first place?

- Sure I told you before, said Conn. - Did I not tell you?

- Naw. What?

- He's been drivin Josie Rabbitt to Confession in Portglenone abbey once a month for the last twenty years. Josie can't drive.

- Aw, right. I remember you tellin me now, said Myles. - So Josie doesn't trust the seal of confession in Derry then?

- Josie knows the priests in Derry will forgive, said Conn - but he's not too sure about them forgettin.

- A wise man, said Myles.

- Pat! shouted Conn. - Is that Guinness ready yet?

Pat closed his eyes and slapped his forehead.

- My God, he said. - I must be takin that Alts - what d'you call it? Alts somethin. What d'you call it, Myles?

- I'd say you must have it, answered Myles. - That's always the sign, Pat. If you don't remember the name of it, you've got it.

The lace curtains lifted and fell from the breath of a sudden breeze and little girls rhymed the same skipping game over and over.

> *I'm a sailor home from sea*
> *To see if you will marry me.*
> *Will you marry,*
> *Marry marry marry,*
> *Will you marry me?*

Melanie stretched out her hand and touched him.

- You're still wearing that thing, she said.

He edged the condom off and slipped it under the bed.

- It's funny you using that. Mickey never uses anything.

- He should, said Conn. He closed his eyes and gave a long lethargic yawn.

- Why should he? she asked.

Mickey, Mickey, Mickey. She talked about him a lot. Conn could see him. Smug, coddled and stupid. A strutting little shirt button.

- Why should he? she said again. - Sure I'm on the pill.

Suddenly, urgently, she laid her hand on him again.

- Do it now, she whispered. - Now!

*My God. I've just **finished** doing it. What does she think I am?*

She ran hungry fingers through the hairs of his thickly matted chest and stomach and down to his shrunken cock. There she fondled him, hopefully at first, then peevishly until finally she gave up and said - Right. Do it the other way.

It was an order. He shook his mind from thoughts of sleep and began to ease his left hand under her. She raised her arse a little for him and with painstaking softness he probed to the bottom of her spine and back, lingering awhile when he felt her shudder or heard the change in her breath. With his right hand he chafed her knees the way she liked and then caressed her thighs, tipfingering meticulously upwards till he reached the warm moistness that nestled in her silken slit and there, exhausted, he searched for the place again.

When it was over she turned and smiled at him, her green eyes shining, her rust-red hair long and luxuriant on his shoulder and pillow. Then she slid up his side till she was on top of him.

- Hold me tight, old man, she said.

She was soft and beautiful, yet even with the closeness of her sweet swells and cavities she might just as well have been a sack of spuds for all the pleasure he felt. His stomach tickled and twitched with their fluids but there was a lassitude and near numbness in him and he wished she would let him sleep. His oxters were clabbered in sweat and the nylon undersheet that had earlier given off sparks was now gathered in hard ridges beneath his left shoulder blade. Cotton sheets in future. Gentle crushed cotton like you get in underpants.

- I'd rather have you than Mickey, she said.

- That's good.

- Just good?

- Naw, that's great.

He kissed her on the lips and eyelids.

- Mickey just charges in so he does, she said. - And then he's away looking for his cigarettes and next thing you know he's sleeping. He hasn't a clue.

Conn liked hearing this but her tone told more than her words. Mickey was the main event. *Maybe it's a strutting stud that he is.*

- What age are you, Conn? You never told me.

- I'm thirty-two and some months, he said, smiling wearily. - Sure you know that.

- No, really. What age are you?

- I told you. Thirty-two and some months.

- You're my dirty old uncle, she said. - You're taking advantage of me.

She's so young, he thought as she moved on him. So superb. She's going to kill me.

- What's your favourite colour? she asked.

- What?

- What's your favourite colour? Mine's lilac.

- I don't know. Purple.

- Purple's the masculine of lilac. Did you know that?

- Naw.

- What's your favourite film? Mine's *To Kill a Mockingbird*.

- I don't know. Listen, Melanie. I've had a rough week.

34

Could we go to sleep for awhile?

Her lower lip trembled a little and then quickly jutted out in anger.

- You don't care about me!

- Please. Don't say that.

- You don't care about me! she repeated and hit his shoulder with the side of her fist.

- A girl said that to me one time, said Conn, - and she ended up nearly destroyin me.

- Who is she? Do I know her?

- Ah, she's long gone. I don't even know where she is.

- Did she break your heart?

- She did. I flipped over it. I was nearly goin to kill myself.

- You mean a mental breakdown?

- Aye.

The anger had gone and a film of mist was forming in the shine of her almond eyes.

- Were you in Gransha hospital?

- I was. But I got over it.

Why am I telling her this?

- Poor Conn. Do you still fancy her a bit?

- I do not. Not anymore. It's nearly like it happened to somebody else.

- Nearly but not quite.

- Nearly but not quite.

- What's her name?

- It doesn't matter. It was a long time ago.

- What's her name? Tell me.

- Lucia.

Melanie slipped down his side onto her back and lay looking at him.

- Mickey knows about us, she said.

- What!

- I didn't tell him. But he knows I'm with somebody else at the weekends.

- How did he find out? Sure we never leave the house together.

- He phoned my mother's last Saturday and she told him I wasn't staying there. She didn't know, you see. She thought I was with him and he thought I was with her.

- So what did you tell him?

- I didn't tell him anything. I told him he must have picked my mother up wrong. But he knows. He doesn't know who you are yet but he knows.

She half rose and began struggling with the woollen blankets.

- I'm going to the toilet, she said.

She pulled at the bedclothes, seeming for a moment to swim away from him, her little arse suddenly in the air, two pink ladies side by side in an autumn orchard.

- Don't be going to sleep on me now, she called as she walked to the bathroom door. She turned to look at him.

- You hear me? she said.

Her breasts shone pale and lovely in the curtained light and her nipples glistened from the damp of their bodies. She had her hands lowered now, covering the place between her legs, and he felt a dull exasperation that he couldn't give her the treatment she was entitled to. A girl like her was made for

36

endless love. In his daydreams it was always the same. She lay impaled, bucking and thrusting, filled to overflowing, yelling for more.

The bathroom door clicked shut. With a great effort he smoothed the ridges from the undersheet and then went limp, his eyelids heavy and feeble. Maybe I'll be ready for her when I waken, he thought. Maybe I can make it just right.

A little girl cried outside.

- You said I could skip. You told me. You promised.

- I said no such thing. Run away home to your ma.

The skipping rope slapped the road and a new chant began.

> *If you give me a silver spoon*
> *To feed my baby in the afternoon*
> *I won't marry,*
> *Marry marry marry,*
> *I won't marry you.*

He heard the click and then the footstep. As Melanie came forward she saw his open-mouthed gaze and immediately cupped her hands in front of her again. It was an alluring thing, this covering of herself from his eyes. She climbed back into bed and lay shivering.

- Warm me up, she said.

He took her in his arms and held her hard against him.

- We'll do it again after dinner, won't we? she said.

- Aye.

- We'll sleep now, she said. - Okay?

- Okay.

She turned away from him and almost immediately began

to snore, throbbing like a contented cat.

I'll get as much as I can with her. Save it all for Confession when she dumps me, when she's paid me in full. Tip it into God's skip in one go. She doesn't think about guilt. She doesn't have any guilt. No baggage, no fear, just the simple expectation of love. No heaven, no hell, one life, one death. How did it start, this freedom from conscience? To lie with whoever you can and not be afraid. I'll have to tell Myles about her. He's like Mickey, he knows there's someone but he doesn't know who it is. What an arrangement. Secret. Fantastical. And temporary. Yes, it's temporary all right. She'll stop the sighing when she wants me away. Well, fuck, be fucked and be merry for some Friday soon I'll be back to too much drink in The Drunken Dog.

All Saints were losing with fifteen minutes to go and Conn had two big worries. First, defeat would mean certain relegation and second, he couldn't bear the thought of being put down by Saint Brendan's, the all-conquering school of his nightmares.

Cyril Prendergast, who sometimes seemed to Conn to have an ongoing deal with the devil such was his team's success, stood on the opposite touchline roaring all the wrong things and getting all the right reactions.

- WAKEN UP, SAINT BRENDAN'S! YEEZ ARE PLAYIN LIKE A CROWD OF BIG GIRLS' BLOUSES!

His floppy fair hair flew in his face and his pallid cheeks filled with air. He'd never kicked a ball in his life and he managed the best school team in Derry.

- BURY THEM! he bawled. - IF YEEZ DON'T BURY THEM NOW YEEZ WON'T BE GETTIN THE NICE NEW GYMSLIPS I PROMISED YEEZ!

The Saint Brendan's boys responded as if spurred by the most inspirational coach in the world. They surged forward for the killer goal. All Saints obliged by falling back, trying to hold on to their one-goal deficit.

Prendergast was bad enough but Conn also had the enemy within standing not five metres away. Once upon a time Gus Hazlitt had been the stronger one of the partnership. His great knowledge of football had made All Saints the most feared primary school in town. Year after year and glory after glory Conn and Gus had dovetailed happily until the night of the fateful dinner dance in Altnagelvin nurses' home when Gus met the Holy Spirit. She wore an off-white three-quarter length polyester dress with matching alice band and she went by the name of Pippa Gurney. Gus met her and married her and never looked back. This wasn't surprising for behind him were serpents in the night, multitudinous mounds of vomit and the big black panther with the yellow eyes. However, the Spirit's gain was hard on All Saints for Gus had gradually lost interest in winning matches, insisting instead that participation was the whole point. And lately he'd got to toying with the theory that winning was a corrupting experience and losing was the road to enlightenment. Cyril Prendergast thought this was a howl. Cyril had a way of laughing that was only slightly less beguiling than a mangy dog's final whine and he'd laughed at some length when he told Conn that Gus's philosophy was a cop-out. Gus no longer had the stomach for football, opined Cyril, and was now operating as talent scout for the Holy Spirit which even in this world of cynical souls was a doddle compared to co-managing a team whose best days were behind it.

- COVER UP! shouted Conn. - PATRICK, MARK UP! NOW!

Gus's defection had also hit The Drunken Dog. There were drinkers there who still recalled Gus's raucous and rumbustious account of how the rugby ball had got its shape. The story had been retold many times since the Saturday before the night of the Damascene dance but never with the same charisma, panache or pure vulgarity that had characterised Gus's closing performance.

He'd been quiet for most of the match, confining himself to the occasional comment about the weather, but now he began to move towards Conn with a purposeful stride.

What's he going to say? Maybe, just this one time, he's going to suggest some tactical change that will swing the match our way.

He stopped beside Conn and gazed thoughtfully at the River Foyle rolling lazily behind the Daisyfield.

- I was just tryin to remember somethin, he said. - Who was it that came out with the expression: all that it takes for evil to triumph is for good men to do nothin?

Conn stared at him.

- I'm almost sure it was said by a Jew shortly after Hitler came to power, said Gus. - You don't remember, do you?

Conn shook his head.

40

- BILLY, GET BACK INTO POSITION! he roared. - WE'RE WIDE OPEN DOWN THE LEFT!

Billy didn't do as he was told. Instead, with tears in his eyes he walked towards Conn and Gus.

- Sir, he said when he arrived. - Tommy Breslin called me a grunter. Sir, there's not enough studs on my boots and I'm slippin all the time. It's not my fault.

- Billy, said Conn. - Look, you're playin well. Stay out of the mud as much as you can. Now go. We can still win this match.

- Mister Doherty's right, said Gus. - Go back in there and play the way we know you can.

Billy looked at Gus, an expression of confused gratitude on his face. He started to run onto the pitch.

- And Billy! called Gus.

Billy stopped and turned.

- I want you to enjoy the rest of this match, win or lose, continued Gus. - Get in there and enjoy it. There are more important things than winnin.

Billy's forehead furrowed.

- Go now, shouted Conn.

Billy went.

- He's a good lad, said Gus. - But, as I was goin to say there, I think the Jew got it wrong.

- MARK UP! screamed Conn. - MARK UP, EVERYBODY!

It was too late. The ball skidded about the All Saints goal area and a wispy little Saint Brendan's boy tapped it into the net. Two nil.

- You know why he's wrong? asked Gus.

- STEADY UP, ALL SAINTS! roared Conn. - JACKIE, YOU PULL BACK INTO MIDFIELD. JOHN AND MARK, PLAY UP FRONT.

- He's wrong, explained Gus, - because if men do nothin in the face of evil, they can't be good men. Good men don't do nothin.

- What? said Conn.

- You see, it's a contradiction. It's what you would call an oxymoron.

- TOMMY BRESLIN! screamed Conn. - IF I HEAR YOU SLAGGIN BILLY AGAIN YOU'RE OFF. DO YOU HEAR ME? OFF!

- Sir yes, called Tommy.

- Tell us this, said Gus. - Are you applyin?

- I don't think so, said Conn.

- You should. You'd get it.

- Myles is tryin to get me to apply but I don't know.

- What's Myles doin? Did he ever go back to teachin?

- He did not. Sure if he'd gone back he wouldn't have got a fraction of the compensation he did get.

- It was a ridiculous settlement, said Gus. - He's drinkin our money. You know that, don't you? It's more rates and taxes for you and me to pay.

- What are you talkin about? snapped Conn. - He was entitled to every penny of it. Sure those soldiers nearly left him brain damaged.

- He looks all right to me, said Gus.

- And, by the way, why don't you start complainin about

your taxes bein used to fund the British occupation of this place? It's your money that's helpin to pay for the plastic bullets, you know.

- Render onto Caesar, answered Gus. He looked up at the sky.

- I think there's more rain comin.

He zipped up his anorak and stared at the grey waters of the Foyle.

- Tell us this, he said. - Is he still a non-practisin Catholic?

- Naw, said Conn. - MOVE UP, ALL SAINTS! DON'T LEAVE A GAP IN THE MIDDLE! Naw, sometimes he claims he's a practisin humanist. He says he reckons if he practises enough he'll have it right by about the year two thousand.

Gus hmnphed.

- He hasn't changed then. Still comin out with that sort of flippancy. He obviously thinks it's the sign of a great mind to be rudderless.

- YOU'RE OFFSIDE, DECLAN. MOVE OUT!

Conn's shout was halfhearted. The game was almost up.

- It's all this James Joyce stuff, said Gus. - Is he still a Joyce fanatic?

- He is.

- He read somewhere about Joyce crawlin in the gutter stewed to the gills and he reckons livin the same way gives him some sort of intellectual affinity. I've no time for him at all.

Conn looked at his watch.

- We're goin to be relegated, he said.

43

- I wouldn't worry. It'll be the makin of us.

- What do you mean? We'll be the laughin stock of Derry. All Saints in the second division!

- You know what it's like? said Gus. - Did you ever read anythin about Islam? You know, the religion.

- A bit, here and there.

- Well, it's very much misunderstood. The word Islam means surrender, you know.

- Right enough?

- Oh aye. They have a period of fastin called Ramadan and the idea of it is to surrender their self-interest so that they can appreciate real poverty and hunger.

- Aw aye. Right.

- The whole idea of Islam is based on equality. That's why all these so-called Islamic governments persecute real Muslims. Most of them are manipulated by the two big powers, you see, so they're not really Islamic.

- I didn't know that, said Conn. - But what's it all got to do with All Saints bein relegated?

- Humblin yourself, explained Gus. - That's what it's got to do with it. It's a character-formin process.

- So are you thinkin of movin over to Islam then? asked Conn.

- Now Conn. But seriously, I think we've all got somethin to learn from other religions. Our minds have to stay open.

- But not to humanism.

- Not to humanism.

He suddenly put his hand on Conn's arm.

- Listen, he said. - I just want to tell you that I really think

44

you should apply.

- I'd never get it.

- Yes you would. Look, I don't have the same politics as you but I still think you're the one they should appoint.

Conn sniffed.

- That's a goodun, he said. - I don't even know what my politics are and you don't agree with them.

- You support Sinn Féin, don't you?

- What are you talkin about? I don't even vote. I think what the IRA's doin is a disaster. Just because I try to understand why they're doin it doesn't mean I agree with any of it.

- There's a fine line.

- Aye, but there is a line, said Conn.

The final whistle blew and Cyril Prendergast shouted - READY, SAINT BRENDAN'S! THREE CHEERS FOR ALL SAINTS! HIP HIP!

- HOORAY! came the gleeful chorus.

- HIP! HIP!

- HORRAY!

- HIP! HIP!

- HORRAY!

The All Saints boys slunk slowly towards the touchline. Cyril easily overtook them and shook hands with Conn and Gus.

- Commiserations, he smiled.

- Well done, said Gus.

- Good victory, said Conn. - I hope you go on now and win the league.

What an utter bastard.

- Don't talk to me about religion! snorted Myles.

Nobody was talking to him about religion. Nobody was talking to him about anything. He was sitting alone in his corner of The Drunken Dog, the Irish News spread out in front of him.

- Careful with that whiskey, Myles, said Pat. - You're goin to spill it if you don't watch.

- I need somebody to explain somethin to me, said Myles, folding the paper and throwing it onto another table.

- What's that?

- How can those rabbis get away with tellin the Jews they're not allowed to turn on the central heatin on a Saturday?

- The rabbis don't say that do they? said Pat. - The cigarette machine isn't workin there, Danny. Here, I've ones behind the bar. What kind do you want?

- It says it right there in the paper, said Myles. - Do you know that if a Jew does a bit of cookin or switches on the light on the Sabbath day he's breakin the fourth commandment?

- What's electrics got to do with honourin your father and mother? asked Danny. - Silk Cut. Give us twenty would you?

- I'm talkin about the Torah, explained Myles, - not the Irish catechism. The fourth commandment of the Torah says to keep the Sabbath day holy. And the rabbis say that means no electrics.

- My God, said Pat. - I wouldn't like to be a Jew.

- You could always eat out, said Danny. - Spend your

Saturdays in The Drunken Dog.

Pat leaned on the bartop, chin in hand.

- You're talkin about the Jews. Sure I remember the time we used to have to fast from midnight if we wur goin to Holy Communion the nixt mornin.

- Aye, the pope changed all that, didn't he? Said Danny.

Myles laughed bitterly.

- Don't talk to me about that man. Sure he won't even allow women to be priests. And you know why?

- Why? asked Danny.

- Because Christ never had any women apostles. Did you ever hear of the like of it? Christ didn't have a three-litre Ferrari either and there was never any word of the pope bannin *them*.

- You know what I think? said Danny. - It's bad enough tellin your sins to a man. But do you see if I had to tell them to a woman, I think I'd become a Hindu.

- I'll tell you now about Hinduism, said Myles.

- Naw, please don't, begged Pat, joining his hands in prayer.

- Tell me somethin, Myles, said Danny. - Where did you suddenly get this great respect for women?

- What do you mean? demanded Myles. - I always respected women.

Pat laughed.

- Then how come you give those two that come in here on a Thursday such a bad time?

- Is it the two great whites you're talkin about? snorted Myles.

47

- Those aren't women. Those are fucken maneaters.

- I think I know the two you're on about, said Danny. - The wee one's a real bomb. What's this you call her?

- Caressa Ball? suggested Myles.

- God forgive you, said Pat. He studied a damp patch at the corner of the bartop and wiped it slowly. - I know the one. Her name's on the tip of me tongue.

- Felicia Alcocks? ventured Myles.

- That's enough outa you, said Pat. His eyes brightened and he snapped his fingers. - She's Doherty! The two of them's Doherty. Same name as meself.

- You don't say? said Myles. He looked up at the clock. - Tell us, what night's this?

- Monday. Why are you astin?

- Naw, I'm just wonderin about Conn, if he's comin tonight. He's been missin in action these past two or three weekends and I'm startin to git worried about him.

Danny was staring at the television.

- Hey, did yous hear what your man on the news just came out with?

- What? asked Myles.

- He said, "There was no bomb in the car bomb". I swear. That's what he said.

- What channel's that? asked Myles.

- ITN, said Danny.

The door opened and Conn came in.

- Hey, Conn, called Danny. - Do you know what the newsreader's after sayin about the car belongin to the three IRA ones in Gibraltar?

48

- What? asked Conn.

- He said, "There was no bomb in the car bomb". What do you think of that?

- What can you say? said Conn.

- I doubt they were up to no good, said Pat.

- What the fuck are you talkin about? snapped Myles.

- They wurn't there for the sun, wur they? said Pat. - Three IRA together in a British colony?

- Reconnaissance probably, said Conn.

Myles' face had become red with anger.

- The SAS were flown in to murder them. Thatcher's orders. Twelve with guns against a girl and two men that hadn't even a penknife between them.

- You really think it came from the top? asked Danny.

- Course it did.

- **Oi!**

- **Yes?**

- **That's libellous.**

- **What's libellous?**

- **Saying the orders came from Thatcher.**

- **But it's true.**

- **It may well be true but you can't write it. She'll take you to court and win.**

- **It stays. Writing's about telling the truth.**

- **What's the truth?**

- **The truth? The truth is what's true.**

- **Can you prove the order came from Thatcher? If not you could end up in jail. That woman has access to the best barristers in Britain.**

- The publicity will make the book a bestseller. I'll be famous.

- They'll probably put you in with an eighteen stone sodomite —

- Sod the whole lot of them! Some of us writers still have principles. We may be a dwindling band but —

- whose every organ is proportionate to his body weight.

- Right. Let me see. How about this then?

Myles' face had become red with anger.

- The SAS were flown in to murder them, he growled.

- Do you think the order came from Thatcher? asked Danny.

- Well, let's say the killers knew she wouldn't be losin any sleep over it, answered Myles.

- Spot on. I like the nice touch of innuendo there.

- Okay. Okay. Where was I?

- Something about a dwindling band of writers?

- Yes, I've got it now.

- the killers knew she wouldn't be losin any sleep over it, answered Myles.

- Could you do us a pint of Guinness there, Pat? asked Conn.

- And a wee Jameson for Myles.

- Will surely.

- And you know who else won't be losin any sleep over it? continued Myles, his face now flushed to a dull crimson.

- Who? said Danny.

- The Catholic bishops, that's who.

- Aw now, complained Pat. - You shouldn't be sayin them sorta things. It's not lucky.

Myles gave him a withering look and turned to Conn. - What was it James Joyce wrote? he said.

- Books? suggested Conn.

Myles turned his face to the ceiling, closed his eyes and recited loudly:

O Ireland, my one and only love,
Where Christ and Caesar are hand in glove.

He looked at the others and said - That's what Joyce wrote and he wasn't wrong about much.

- Sorry. Excuse me.

- I don't believe this. What is it now?

- At the risk of being taken out I'd like to draw your attention to something else.

- Draw away. And make it quick.

- That quote from Joyce. You've just infringed copyright.

- No I haven't. Ha! Jimmy wrote that more than seventy years ago. I can quote all I want. The law says copyright expires after seventy years.

- Oh, so it's Jimmy now, is it?

- It is.

- Well, I hope for your sake Stevie and his lawyers don't take offence.

- Stevie? Stevie who?

- Stevie Joyce, Jimmy's grandson. He holds the rights for all time. And he's not a man to trifle with.

- I thought he was dead.

- Nope. He's alive and kicking the bejasus out of people like you.

- You're not serious!

- Listen. Don't get me wrong here. I'm very happy with the book so far. It definitely shows promise. But do you see if Stephen Joyce so much as smells those fifteen words, he'll take you for all you've got. And that'll be the end of the two of us.

- I wouldn't worry about it. He'll never read my book.

- You think not? Let me tell you something now. Mister Stephen reads everything. *Every*thing. His guiding principle is this. If two or more words belonging to Granda James are gathered together in somebody else's name they constitute an unlawful assembly. This may be hard for you to accept but Stevie and his legal team have given an entirely new meaning to the term proofreading.

- Mmm. Tell me something, Myles. Have you been to many pubs in Derry?

- I don't know. You tell me.

- The fact is, most of the pubs in Derry have those fifteen words plastered all over their walls.

- Really?

- Yip. You know the poster showing famous Irish writers and quotes from things they wrote?

- Never heard of it.

- You must know it. There's one behind the bar in The Drunken Dog.

- I've never seen it.

- Well, it's there now. Anyway, my point is, if Stephen

Joyce sues me, he's also going to have to take on nearly every publican in Derry and possibly in Ireland.

- Ah.

- And it just so happens I'm friendly with the vice-chairman of the Northwest Vintners' Association. Ha! And there's something else. Johnny Jameson and Sons are behind the distribution of the posters so I reckon we should be able to get some help there. No, somehow I don't think Mister Stephen will want to take on that Jameson crowd. No one knows better than him what they did to his granda.

- And then it'll be even Stephen?

- Very good, Myles. I wish I'd said that.

- You will. Trust me. You will.

Danny stared at his watch for a moment and then jumped off the stool.

- Jesus, look at the time, he said.

He went to the door and called back - I'll see yous all later.

- Right, Danny, said Pat. - Take it easy.

- That was quick, said Conn. - Why's he away so early?

- He has to put the wee ones to bed, said Pat. - His babysitter goes at half nine on a Monday.

Myles cleared his throat.

- How do you reckon he's gettin on? he asked.

Pat came over and sat down at the table. He leaned towards the other two and they recoiled slightly as the foetid blast of trapped food assailed their senses.

- He's up and down, said Pat. - You know the way it is.

- It must be rough, said Conn.

- He's had a bad time, said Pat. - Poor fella.

- It's still hard to take in, said Conn.

Pat shifted his chair up against the table, brought his head closer to Myles and Conn and lowered his voice.

- I'm worried about him, to tell you the truth. It's comin near the first anniversary and I don't know what he's goin to do.

- When you're talkin to him you'd hardly know anythin happened, said Conn.

- If you'd been with me last Christmas Eve you'd have known all right, said Pat.

- How d'you mean? asked Myles.

- I came across him about half two in the mornin just after I finished closin up here. I was goin past Free Derry Corner and I saw him wanderin about in his pyjamas in the freezin cold. I says, "Are you all right there, Danny?" and he comes over to me and says, "Pat, you didn't see Mary about, did you?" Jesus. She was dead nearly nine months. I says to him, "Listen, Danny, what are you doin out here? You should be in the house." "She nivir came back", he says to me. "She went out shoppin in the Richmond Centre and she nivir came back. I can't get the wee ones settled. She's very late, Pat."

- Christ, breathed Myles.

- I got him back to the house and I stayed with him awhile. The wains wur sleepin, thank God, and he sat talkin about the time him and Mary lived in a caravan down in Malin Head before the first one was born. But then he started again about her not bein back yit and he kept lookin at the door as if he was expectin her to walk in any minute.

- It should never have happened, said Myles, shaking his head.

54

- Openin fire in a place like that. The ones the Ra sent out weren't up to the job.

Pat shoved his chair back and got up.

- If you ast me, he said, - the Ra wurn't worried who got it. I don't care how much you hate the troops. You don't start a gun battle in Shipquay Street.

The bar door suddenly opened and three men wearing Star Trek outfits came tumbling in.

- How about yous? enquired Pat as they stood uncertainly in the middle of the floor. - Tell us this and tell us no more. Which wan of yous is Spock?

- Who do you think? answered a tall stern-looking man with pointy ears.

He looked around him, puzzled.

- Is this where the Trekkies' convention is supposed to be? he asked.

- Upstairs, said Pat. - Just go back outside there and it's the door with the arrow on it that says UPSTAIRS. You can't miss it.

- You'll be Doctor McCoy then, said Conn to a paunchy little individual sporting an outsize stethoscope.

The man swayed slightly and said - Very obshervant.

- I must say I like your get-ups, said Pat. - But I don't see Captain Kirk. Where's Captain Kirk?

- He's comin later, answered a large man wearing a tartan kilt that didn't quite match the rest of his attire. - He had to do overtime.

- Captain Slog, said Conn.

- Would yous like a wee dram here before yous take off?

55

asked Pat.

- No thanks, answered Spock. - I think we'd better get movin.

- Right. Good luck, called Pat and the three filed out.

Myles sat shaking his head with amused contempt.

- Spacers, he said.

- I'll tell you somethin though, said Conn. - That's still one of the best series on TV.

- Star Track? said Pat. – It's very good right enough.

He screwed up his eyes and stared at Myles as if trying to place him.

- You did a bit of actin in your day, didn't you? he asked.

- You're goin back a few years there, said Myles.

- Aye, you wur in a play in Saint Columb's Hall the time of internment, went on Pat. - Sure I mind hearin about it and all. Some patriotic thing.

- That's right, said Myles. - *The Trial of Robert Emmet*. It had a very short run.

- Just the one night, wasn't it? said Conn, smiling.

- One night only, nodded Myles. - It didn't go down too well. There were two or three things thrown if I remember right.

- You don't say? said Pat. - I nivir heard about that now.

He produced a stack of ash trays from behind the bar and went to the tables with them.

- Yeah, said Myles. - You know how Emmet made a great speech from the dock before the Brits took him out and executed him? Well, the audience in Saint Columb's got so mad when they saw the judge reachin for the black cap that he had to get the jury to reconsider. And guess what?

- They acquitted him, said Conn.

- That didn't happen. Did it? asked Pat.

- It did, said Myles. - Best piece of improvisation in the history of theatre. Unfortunately we had to go on tour right away.

- I don't recall that now, said Pat.

- Do you not? said Myles, looking surprised. - We were all over the country so we were. The best reception we had was up in Carrickfergus, actually.

- Carrickfergus? Is that not a very Protestant place? asked Pat.

- Is it, said Myles. - We did it in an Orange hall too.

- You're jokin! said Pat. - And how did it go down?

- It went down a bomb, answered Myles. - The audience were with us all the way—

- Now hold on a minute, said Pat.

- but we managed to shake them off about six miles out the road.

He roared laughing.

- Yous wurn't in Carrickfergus, said Pat. - I don't believe that.

The door creaked slowly open behind him and framed in the darkness stood a girl.

- Oh sorry, she said. - This must be the wrong place. I was lookin for the Trekkies.

She was slim, slightly dressed and not more than seventeen. She had a face from heaven and wine-red boots that clung to her thighs.

- Upstairs, love, said Myles.

She looked around the room, confused. Pat put his hand on her shoulder.

- Naw. Outside, dear, he said. - It's the first door on your left as you go out. The one with the arrow on it. It says UPSTAIRS. You can't miss it.

- Thanks, she said.

Six eyes followed her intently as she turned and left. There was silence for a few seconds and then Myles asked - Was that a skirt she was wearin?

- It looked like a belt to me, sighed Pat.

- To boldly go, said Conn, - where no man has gone before.

- You reckon? said Myles. - I'd say from the look of her there've likely been one or two wee steps for mankind already.

- Aw now, boys, said Pat. - Less of that.

Myles sat down and threw back the end of his whiskey.

- You wouldn't do us a Jameson and a stout there, would you, Pat?

- Up and comin, answered Pat.

Myles revolved the empty glass in his hand and considered it.

- Sure that's about all we're fit for, he said sadly.

- Speak for yourself, said Conn. - All I'd need is for somebody to beam me up.

- Yous are the great men for talkin, said Pat. He looked at his watch. - I'm wonderin about the table quiz crowd. They should have been here by now.

As he spoke a grey billow of cigarette smoke entered the

bar. Behind it came a large group of seventysomething women, all with big hair and metallic blue rinses.

Myles turned to them and shouted - Here's wan for you lassies. What's the largest lake in the world?

There was a rush of throaty baritone responses and they were all the same.

- The Caspian Sea!

Myles said to Conn - Trick question. It's a goodun, isn't it?

- It used to be, said Conn. - The dogs in the street know it now.

- Not to speak of the bitches in the bar, said Myles.

Mister McGrotty tapped his pencil on the office desk and went back to 5 across.

Put a bolt on the horse's compartment before he can do the bolting.

Nine letters. Third letter... mm... mmm... What's the third letter?

There was a sharp knock on the door. The headmaster quickly folded the Derry Journal and slid it into the bottom drawer.

- Yes? he called.

Brian Kelly edged his head in and said - Is it okay if I have a word with you?

- Surely, Brian. Come in. Sit down.

- I came to see you because I'm feelin a bit hard done by.

- Don't be standing there all stiff like that, said Mister McGrotty. - Here. Sit down.

Brian lowered himself heavily into the chair.

- You know I applied for that job in Star of the Sea Primary last month, he said.

- Yes?

- It only carries a Scale Two allowance but it would be a step up from what I'm on now.

- Yes?

- Well, the short list is out and I'm not on it.

- I see.

Mister McGrotty shifted his pencil from hand to hand. He noticed that the bottom drawer was half open and slammed it shut. Brian stared at him, his face gathered in a knot.

- It really isn't a case of the money, he said. - It's... it's the indignity. I've been teachin eighteen years and they didn't even call me for interview. But it seems they've shortlisted Rory McAdams.

- Really?

- Yeah. I taught him in this school fifteen years ago. Got him through the eleven plus.

- Mm.

The headmaster pulled a blank pad closer to him and drew a small five-cornered star in the corner of it.

- I can understand your frustration, Brian, but that's the way these things go sometimes. I've been told that Rory McAdams is a very talented young teacher.

- Look, said Brian. His voice trembled a little. - I've been teachin all these years. I've worked hard, I've been conscientious and nobody has ever found fault with me—

- That's all true and I understand your annoyance.

- and I'm wonderin what I have to do to get promotion in this job.

- All I can say is, keep applying.

- I *have* been applyin for years and not once was I ever shortlisted.

The words came out as if they'd been dredged from deep inside him.

- What do I have to do to get noticed? I'm not goin to lick arses, if that's what they want.

He stopped, lips taut, wondering if he'd gone too far.

Mister McGrotty looked straight ahead. His eyes were fixed on a large discoloured area of the door just behind Brian's head. His pencil drummed the pad like a metronome. Suddenly his features loosened a little and he leaned forward.

- But Brian, he said. - You have to.

- What? What do you mean?

- Listen, said Mister McGrotty. - We're both grown-up. Everybody who gets promoted in this job gets that promotion on merit. It's just that there are different kinds of merit.

Brian brought the palm of his hand down hard on his knee.

- I couldn't do that! he snapped. - I couldn't do that and look at myself again.

Mister McGrotty raised his shoulders to his ears and then let them fall slowly with an air of sad tolerance.

- I hope you'll forgive my frankness, Brian, but this is the real world.

- These are Catholic schools, Brian said hoarsely. - How *can* they?

- I repeat. The real world.

The headmaster mechanically counted away the seconds of silence that followed. He wanted rid of this man and back to the crossword and he was relieved when Brian rose abruptly and went to the door.

- I'll tell you what I'm goin to do, said Brian, standing pale and rigid, half turned, one hand on the door knob. - I'm goin to go to the bishop about this. The bishop's a good man. *He'll* see that I've been…. trampled on.

- Brian, said Mister McGrotty. - I honestly think you should give your mind a chance to settle. After all, it's not long since you'd the terrible loss.

- Now's the time. *Now's* the time. They'll still be able to draw up a new short list.

- Sit down a minute!

Mister McGrotty's tone was suddenly sharp and commanding but Brian stood on, his hand on the knob. His chest felt tight and empty of air and there was a dull ache in his upper back. The knob was slippery from his sweat and the thought came uninvited that he'd have to remember to wipe it dry with his sleeve before he left. The headmaster rose and went over to Brian. He took him firmly by the arm and said quietly - Come on, sit down. There's something I have to tell you.

Brian came slowly away from the door and back to his seat.

Mister McGrotty moved to the radiator behind his desk and stood, gingerly testing his backside on it.

- You've three cousins, he said. - Paddy and Martha and Joan Kelly, all qualified teachers.

- Aye? What about it?

- I'm sure you're aware they walked the streets for years without a job. But do you know why?

- I heard a lot of talk about my Uncle Benny not gettin on with the parish priest. Father O'Halloran, I think it was.

- Your Uncle Benny was at loggerheads with the church for most of the time he was teaching and that was the result. His son and two daughters scraping a living subbing for half their working lives.

Brian breathed out hard through his nose.

- I don't get it, he said. - It's just not right.

- I'm telling you all this for your own good, said Mister McGrotty. He moved away from the radiator and sat down.

- You remember Liam Touhy? he asked.

- What do you mean? Brian said testily. - Sure he was still headmaster here when I started.

- Well. He used to say, "Get the right combination and you're in. Break the code and you're out."

- So that's the real world is it? said Brian and jerked himself up out of the chair.

- Don't get cynical now, said Mister McGrotty. - It's not going to do you any good, you know.

Brian walked to the door and stood with his back to it, rubbing his right sleeve against the knob.

- I have to go, he said. - My class will be comin out of

Music soon.

- Okay. But remember, Brian. If you've any ambitions to better yourself, don't go running to the bishop.

The door snapped open and closed. The headmaster sat staring ahead at the yellowing patch on the panel above the knob. He thought, I must get some painting done. This place is so drab.

He took the newspaper from the drawer and put it back on the desk. His eyes closed and he leaned forward.

Put a bolt on the horse's compartment before he can do the bolting. Nine letters.

After a few moments he opened his eyes.

Third letter probably.... third letter probably r.

- And d'you know the most significant part of the whole episode? said Conn.

- What? said Myles.

- McGrotty thought he was talkin to one of his own. Otherwise he'd never have opened out about the joys of arselickin.

- Ha!

- Brian saw it. He says it hit him like a bolt of lightnin. He says it was like.... What do you call that Joycean thing?

- An epiphany? said Myles brightly.

- An epiphany. Like an epiphany. He was very funny actually. He said to me afterwards, "I sat there and I saw McGrotty's whole life flashin before me."

- I like that. Joyce would be proud of that.

- You wanted to hear him, said Conn. - He said, "Just because I'm a bit of a middle-class wanker that bastard thought I was one of the club."

- And is he not? asked Myles.

- Naw, he's not. He's got this middle-class mentality all right. Very conformist and all. But he's decent.

- Decent.

- Aye, said Conn. - He's got decency. McGrotty wouldn't recognise that commodity if you coated it with Vaseline and shoved it up his arse.

- Pat, shouted Myles. - Put on a Guinness for Conn there, would you. And a wee half for me.

- Up and comin.

- There was somethin else Brian told me, said Conn, - and I'm workin out what to do about it.

- What?

- The same day as that happened Father Doonican came into his classroom for a chat. In the middle of it he asked Brian who he thought should get the principal's job in All Saints. Brian said, "I don't think Conn Doherty's applyin but he'd be my choice if he was." And Doonican said, "He's no good. He'd be a dangerous influence on the children. He'd destroy the school."

- You're tellin me this actually happened?

- It happened.

- Jesus. Who is this priest anyway?

- Patrick Doonican. He's the school's spiritual director.

- He must be very stupid, said Myles.

- He's that all right. And arrogant as well.

- You've got him over a barrel, Conn.

- I know. But I have to handle it right.

Myles got up and went to the bar.

- For Christ's sake, Pat, he shouted. - Are you boycottin me or what?

Pat wasn't there. But his voice came faintly from the far end of the lounge.

- What is it, Myles? What is it?

The voice moved closer. Then he appeared at the archway behind the bar.

- Is it a drink you're lookin for?

- Drink? Not at all. I was just wonderin if you could give me the long range weather forecast for next summer.

- Weather forecast? You serious? This isn't the BBC, you know.

- Exactly. This is a pub. And I ordered a drink ten minutes ago. What sort of a head have you anyway?

- Aw I'm sorry, Myles, said Pat. He scrambled for the whiskey. -Here you are.

Myles snorted and carried his drink to the table.

- Honest to Christ, he whispered. He turned to Conn.

- But you were sayin there about this man Doonican. Tell me somethin. What's with all the bad-mouthin anyway? Did you and him cross swords or what?

- Not at all, answered Conn. - Anytime I was ever speakin to him I was always dead civil. Naw, when he comes to the school he spends most of his time in McGrotty's office. That's where he got his opinion of me from.

- Brilliant! McGrotty's in shit. He's not supposed to have any input in the selection.

- I know, said Conn. - He's crossed the line.

- Tell me about that. Why does he hate you so much?

- I suppose it's because I stand up to him.

- And does nobody else?

- Not really. Some of them just want a peaceful life and the rest are scared of him.

- And why are you not scared?

- I think I am deep down, said Conn. - He taught me in Saint Brendan's when I was wee and my instinct now is not to let him intimidate me anymore. It would be more than my pride could take.

- Defence mechanism.

- I suppose.

- So what are you goin to do? asked Myles.

- I'm goin to report Doonican to the chairman. Father Babb. Brian's given me the go-ahead.

- What about Josie Rabbitt. He's Mister Big isn't he?

- He is. That's an idea. I may go to him too.

- Although, said Myles, - it's a bit like goin to the godfather to complain about the Mafia.

- It is, agreed Conn. - But what can you do?

- Would you not go to your union?

- Brian says he couldn't face the whole legal thing. I wasn't able to get him to go that far.

- Ah God, said Myles. - Sure he'll never get over his wife.

- I know.

They didn't speak for a minute, looking without interest at

advertisements showing on television.

- Jesus, Conn, you could take McGrotty and Doonican to the cleaners.

- I could and I can't, said Conn. - But I didn't tell you. The whole thing got me so mad I'm applyin for the job.

- That's great. Great. They'll have to give it to you now. Conn laughed.

- Do you think so? he said. - Tell me, are you still gettin the toy truck from Santa this year?

- Maybe you're right.
Conn looked up at Pat.

- What's wrong with that black cow? he asked.

- She's calfin as we speak, said Pat. He went to the half filled Guinness. - I'm sorry, Conn. I got distracted there. That bloody TV would put you to loss.

Myles took a sheet of paper and a biro from his inside pocket and did some scoring and scribbling. He read over it and laughed.

- This is a wee thing I wrote last night, he said.

- Right enough, said Conn. - Is it a poem?

- Not really. It's a wee kind of a....

- A wee kind of a what?

- It's like a religious tract.

- Religious tract? You?

- Yeah, said Myles. - Strangest thing. It just came to me. I think it might have been inspired by one of the four evangelists, actually.

- Very good. Which one was that now?

- John. Wee John. This might turn out to be the new Book

of Revelation.

Pat came over and left a pint of Guinness in front of Conn.

- Thanks Pat.

- Don't mention it son, said Pat and walked through the archway into the lounge.

- Naw, right enough, said Myles. - This thing came to me like a blindin light at twenty past three in the mornin. I was in the middle of one of those really long pees you do sometimes and I was thinkin of Josie Rabbitt and it just came to me.

- Christ. A bit like fallin off your camel on the road to Damascus then?

- Somethin like that, agreed Myles. - Only not as sore.

- So the words just came to you?

- Yeah. I kept sayin to myself, "Why me, Lord?"

- And what did your Lordself say back to you?

- It's funny you askin that, said Myles. - This is about a certain upstandin Derry Catholic builder that spends half the time talkin to God.

- Tell us more, said Conn.

- Do you remember the Last Gospel they used to have at the end of mass before they did away with the Latin?

- I do, said Conn. - In the beginnin was the Word and the Word was with God and the Word was God. The same—

- That'll do, said Myles sharply.

He frowned at Conn with a look of mock concern.

- Sometimes I wonder about you, he said.

- Get on with it.

- Right, said Myles. - That thing you were sayin there now

was the gospel accordin to wee John the evangelist. This one's about big Josie the Falangelist.

- Okay. Shoot.

- *In the beginning was the power, intoned Myles, - and the power was with Josie and the power was Josie. For Josie was God. Well, he thought he was. And who's to say? Maybe he was.*

But lo, a voice from deep within the bowels of his being said onto him: Go redd out the hoors of independent thought from our classrooms and put in the ones that don't know shit and never say no. And if you can't redd the hoors out, at least keep them all on the bottom scale.

Now Josie was a self-willed, self-centred and self righteous man and he had the money that goes with these things. And for this he was held in high regard by many. And in two shakes of a rabbit's tail he was running all the Catholic school boards in town. Truly this was where he came into his own. And his own received him onto their bosoms. And to them he gave leave to kiss his tail. Which they did. And they cried, Yea! Yea, yea! And Josie did say back onto them, Ah! Ahhh, ahhh!.

And so it came to pass that all new Catholic teachers were made by him. And without him were none that were made. For he was the nail, the tooth and the lie. Yet to all who lay before him he gave the chance to become principals. And all who would not lie got hit with the wrecking ball. For Josie was a builder. Did I not tell you? Josie was the biggest builder in town.

And lo, those who were not laid before him were shattered. And they did say about him (him who was): This is he who came after us and then he got us and then he blackballed us and now he is before us, in the power and the glory of his kingdom. For he ranks above all others. Truly he is rank in the eyes of heaven. Yea, yea!

Myles put the sheet of paper back in his pocket.

- There it is, he said. - chapter and verse.

- That was inspired, said Conn. - The best bit of good news I've had all day.

Myles laughed.

- More revelations next week, he said. - Book your copy now.

The table quiz had ended in a dead heat between The Dolldrummers and The Spring Chickens and Hugh the quizmaster was rummaging in his file.

- Hold on, he called out. - Please. I've a list of tie breakers here somewhere.

- Ask them the seven wonders of the world, suggested Danny.

- Give it a rest, shouted Madge Mulcahy of the Dolldrummers. - Everywan knows *them*.

Danny swung round on his stool.

- Right, he shouted. - You name them now, Madge. Just name me one of them.

- The hangin gardens a Babylon.

- Wrong! said Danny and he slapped his thigh. - They're not there anymore. Nul points, Madge.

71

He got down from his stool and stumbled against The Spring Chickens' table.

- Take it easy, said Pat. - Here, Danny. Do you want me to phone you a taxi?

- Nah, no way, said Danny, leaning on Peggy Morrison's shoulder.

- Here! she shouted, her tumbleweed hair bristling. - You get away, Danny Leonard.

- I'm waitin till Myles and Conn are goin, said Danny, stretching his hand in front of him as if feeling the air. - The three of us are gittin a taxi. Right, boys?

- Sure thing, said Myles.

- See? said Danny. - I'll go when I'm good and ready.

Conn came to him and touched his arm.

- Come on over here where we are, he said. - There's plenty of room.

Danny followed Conn to the corner table.

- Good man, he said. - Good man yourself.

He flopped in a chair and called across the room. - Sorry, Peggy. Sorry about that.

Peggy sniffed and then looked up at Hugh.

- Why don't you give us wan off the top of your head? she said.

- I need me winnin drink quick. I shoulda been back in the house twenny minutes ago.

- You're not goin early, Peggy, are you? said Pat.

- Aye, she said. - Willie's in bed with an enlarged prostitute and I have to get back quick.

- Give us wan outa your head now, Hugh, shouted Madge

72

Mulcahy. - What sort of a quizmaster are ye, anyway?

- Listen, said Hugh. - I'd a wile heavy night last night and I'd probbly only end up astin one of the questions I ast yeez already.

Myles got to his feet a little unsteadily.

- Hold on, he said. - How about if *I* ask three multiple choice questions? Me bein a neutral and all. Hatin both teams equally as it were. What do you say, Hugh?

Hugh paused in his search.

- Okay, he said. - If that's all right with the ladies.

Nobody spoke.

- Right, said Myles. - I'll take that as a yes. Now, are you all ready? Pencils out. Teezie

Concannon, stop pickin your nose.

- The cheek! shouted Teezie.

Myles cleared his throat.

- These are all questions about the Republic of Ireland, he announced.

- Is it the football team? asked Susie Doherty.

- Not the football team, said Myles. - The state. The terrible state we're tryin to get into. Now. First question. Out of a population of three and a half million, how many are below the poverty line? Is it *a)* one million, *b)* one and a half million or *c)* two million?

- Wait a minute, shouted Biddy Walker. - What were those three numbers agin?

Myles repeated the numbers and proceeded. - Right. Second question. How much does the Republic of Ireland government spend every year protectin Maggie Thatcher's border from the Republican hordes? Is it *a)* three hundred and fifty million pounds, *b)* four hundred and fifty million pounds or *c)* five hundred and fifty million pounds?

- That's ridiculous, complained Madge Mulcahy. - How would we know that?

- Last question, said Myles firmly. - Why in under fuck are we bustin our balls up here in the North tryin to join up with a bunch of West Britons playin at bein Irish in a Dublin dollhouse? Is it because *a)* we're mad in the head, *b)* we're stupid or *c)* a combination of *a)* and *b)*? Only one answer allowed now.

- God forgive ye, Myles Corrigan, shouted Sadie Shiels. - That's terrible language for a teacher to be usin.

Myles stood swaying gently, a pained expression on his face.

- Who says I'm a teacher? he demanded.- I kicked that habit years ago.

- Ye're a disgrace so ye are, said Peggy Morrison. - To think that my grandchildren—

- Quiet! barked Myles. - If there's not quietness right away I'll keep yous all in after closin.

He pointed an accusing hand at Peggy.

- And we'll have no more scurrilous remarks from the likes of you, Ms Morrison. You know perfectly well I'm not a teacher anymore. I've reformed! Here's me battlin the demons Monday to Friday, week in, week out. And you! Sweet Jesus, woman! Every mornin it's all I can do to stay in my bed when the school bells are ringin. What do you know!

- Hold on, shouted Hugh. - Scrap all that. I've found the

tie breaker.

- Thanks be to God and His Holy Mother, said Sadie. - That man should be put away.

- Who's watchin the wains tonight, Danny? asked Conn.

- Majella, said Danny. - Me sister's daughter.

He swung round from his front seat.

- I was just readin about that girl Mairead Farrell, you know, that the SAS shot out in Gibraltar, he said. - It was in the paper on Sunday about her.

- Aye? said Myles.

- She was a lovely lookin girl, said Danny. - Did any of yous ever see her picture?

- Aye, I saw it, answered Conn.

- There's somethin very good about her, continued Danny.

- Somethin good. D'you see if I hadn't a met Mary, well that's the kinda girl I'd like to have gone out with.

- Right enough? said Conn.

- Aye. You just have to look at her eyes. She's decent. She's ... she's good so she is. That crowd nivir gave her a chance.

He swung back again and looked at the taxi driver.

- Did you ivir see her? he asked.

- I did, said the driver. - I seen her on the TV.

- Brilliant mind too, said Danny. - Very clever. I was readin about her.

He stared out through the taxi window. Reflections of light danced on the glass and on the wet black road.

- I'd say she coulda been anythin she wanted, he went on. - What the fuck was she doin in the IRA anyway?

- Are we goin up the flyover? asked the driver. - Where are yeez all goin anyway?

- This is a terrible country, said Danny.

- Sure don't I know it, said the driver. - Which way?

- Here, said Danny. - Leave me off here. Them two's goin out by the Brandywell. How much do I owe you?

- This one's on me, Danny, called Conn.

- Are you sure?

- Aw aye. This one's on me.

- Thanks, Conn. Thanks very much.

- Not at all. Take care of yourself now.

- All the best, Danny, shouted Myles.

Danny eased himself carefully onto the footpath, slammed the taxi door and gave the roof a heavy slap.

- God look to him, said Myles as they drove on.

There was silence for a few moments and then Conn said

- Those funerals are tomorrow.

- Yeah, said Myles. - I'm goin up, you know.

- I don't believe you.

- Yeah, I'm goin all right. I wasn't goin to go and then this evenin I got mad at the whole lot of them.

- The whole lot of who?

- The whole lot of them. Priests, politicians, media. They're all gangin up on Sinn Féin and the families.

- That's true enough, agreed Conn.

- The only bad thing they have to say about the SAS is that they're playin into the hands of the IRA and Sinn Féin. Not a fucken word about cold-blooded murder.

- The Brits can't win, said Conn. - If they don't shoot people in the back they're lettin them off too lightly and then when they do do it they're handin them propaganda on a plate. Who'd be a Brit?

- Plenty on our side of the house as far as I can see, said Myles.

- Did you hear what Bishop Cathal Daly was sayin last night?

- Naw.

- He said Sinn Féin were keepin the pot boilin by holdin the bodies in Gibraltar.

- But sure that was British bureaucracy, said Conn.

- Bureaucracy my foot! snapped Myles. - The Brits kept them in Gibraltar for eight days just to rub it in.

- You're right there, the driver called back. - And did yeez hear what O'Fiaich and the other cardinals in England and Scotland and Wales are goin to be doin?

- Yeah, I heard, said Myles.

- Naw, tell us, said Conn.

- They're goin to announce to the plain people of Ireland on Paddy's day, said Myles, - that we're all to be good wee boys and girls and try and get on with the Brits. Aw aye. And that Irish violence is wrong. And they're callin that a pastoral!

- What about British violence? said Conn.

- No word about that.

- Christ.

- Christ and Saint Patrick, corrected Myles. - That Jew and that Frenchman must be turnin in their tombs. D'you see if them two came back now, they'd probably be lifted for conspiracy.

- And excommunicated, added Conn.

- Where to now? said the driver.

Myles looked blankly out the window.

- Where are we? he asked. - I can't see a fucken thing with that rain.

- We're just passin the grotto, said the driver.

- Okay, said Myles. - Leave me off at the corner of Bishop Street.

- Are you sure you're wise goin up to Belfast? said Conn.

- How d'you mean?

- The soldiers are goin to attack the funerals. Sure you know that.

- I heard the Ra fired a military salute this evenin already, said the driver. - *They're* not goin to be there.

- That's right, agreed Myles. - And your man Cathal Daly says he was told by some general that the Brits'll be stayin clear too.

- Not worth the paper it's written on, said Conn.

- I think it might be all right, said the driver.

He turned round to Myles.

- Well, this is you.

- Aw, right. Thanks, said Myles. - You're payin, Conn?

- I am.

- Okay. I'll see you then.

He struggled out onto the road. Conn wound down the window.

- Take it easy tomorrow, he called.

Myles didn't hear him. Hunched against the rain and the cold he walked away from them. His face was lit for a

moment in the passing glow of a houselight and then he was
gone.

For a while all he knew was the bleakness. The stupidity of
death and the swarms of sleet that clung to the sides of his
windscreen. Then as he began to negotiate a long slow bend
the sleet drew back and he saw pinholes of sun stealing a way
through and the flickers of the white valley. When he left the
leafbare hedge behind he could see clearly that a light crust of
snow lay across the fields below the Glenshane Pass. A half-
grown lamb leapt twice on all fours leaving small dark doodles
around him. The sun glittered fitfully on the oxbow bend of
a river and sheep with dark faces and dirty stringy wool lay
softening the grass beneath them.

He wanted to stop but he had to get on. Late to bed, late
to rise, what does that make a man? He looked at the clock on
the dashboard. He'd go straight to Milltown cemetery and
miss the requiem mass in Saint Agnes's. That way he'd have
time at Eva's grave before the funerals arrived.

- *I'll see you when all this is over, she said. - You'll come back
soon, won't you? I don't care about the child. Honest. It's you I
want. There.*

- *I love everything you do, she said. - It's better for me if you
know that. You don't hurt me. You couldn't hurt me no matter
what you do.*

*She laughed. - I love you that bad, she said. - I'm a bold girl,
aren't I?*

79

He stood at her Celtic cross. Somewhere to his left were the footfalls and the murmurs of the gathering mourners.

I didn't know enough to know there was never going to be anyone like her again. Each time she took whatever it was she got from me, I owned her for that little time. I remember it. Seeing her face, hearing her voice, feeling her move with me. And when she gave pleasure. When she gave pleasure she looked at me full on and asked the same question always. - Was that all right, Myles? and I said yes and she smiled and said - You're welcome, sir. Come again.

I lost everything. All she lost was the moment she died in. Because her past may as well never have happened. And her future. There was no such thing as her future. What hasn't happened doesn't exist.

But she's gone so long and I'm possessed by her all this time and how is that? The conversation is over, we cannot love, we are finished. Why should I speak to a crumbled skeleton in a crumbled coffin? She's nowhere to be found. That's the downside of reason, the seeing and the not believing. The evil decompose just like Eva and they too turn to a fine dust. No comeuppance, no justice, no sting. Death the leveller.

The bodies of Mairead Farrell and Dan McCann and Sean Savage were late arriving and slow to be buried. Above the buzz of the watching helicopters Myles heard the swish of soil and spades striking stone. The single large grave wasn't ready. His heart sickened to hear the clash of spade and earth. The knife turned a little more for the families.

Thousands of mourners were still walking through the gates of Milltown cemetery. The oppressed and the dispossessed. The faithful, the abandoned, that took their religion from Rome and their politics from home. Myles felt a torn affinity with these people. He could never accept Rome. Many things were possible but not Rome. The princes of the Church that fawn on the exploiters, the persecutors and the murderers and close their doors on the pleading poor. But the poor would always be with them, scraping their pennies and their pounds to give to Peter, so why should they worry?

He decided to stay where he stood. He would pay his respects from there. He looked around at the quiet orderly graves. There wasn't a soldier in sight. It was good to be free of them, for a while at least. He listened to the priests' voices intoning prayers and to the waves of responses undulating in the soft air. Then there was silence except for the hum of a chopper above the motorway behind him and the stuttering rattle of another somewhere beyond the people. To his right a bulky bearded man ran along a path and then stopped to lean against a gravestone, head down. Someone playing hide and seek with his children? He wasn't showing much respect. Myles was about to call him and let him know what was happening when the man suddenly stood upright and threw something in the direction of the mourners. There was an explosion and Myles felt as if his stomach had split. A black belch of clay and smoke rose as high as a house and particles of something showered his hair and shoulders. There were screams and shouts and more explosions. The man stood where he was. He looked assured and relaxed, almost as if he would have taken the time to stop what he was doing for a minute if anyone had cared to strike up a conversation with him. He was only four graves away, as close as a next door neighbour. He took a gun from his pocket. Myles saw this and stumbled along Eva's grave until he was tight against her marble headstone. If the gunman were to turn his head even a little he would probably see Myles' face through the sculpted spaces of the cross. There were three gunshots in quick succession, each with the same sharp crack that Myles knew from twenty years of listening. The man was firing into the crowd of diving running falling people. Then, without hurry, he put the gun away and pulled something from a bag that hung on his shoulder. Like someone playing bowls he leaned forward and rolled one grenade after another towards the parked hearses. The air splintered. The screams grew shriller and, above the screams, hoarse loud voices.

- Get down! Down now!

The man turned and looked into Myles' face and began walking slowly towards him, glancing around as he walked. He raised his gun and the cross shattered open against Myles' chest. The wrong place, the wrong time. Thousands die this way. Myles lowered his head and prayed. He felt the wet heat on one thigh and his bowels began to empty.

- O my God I am heartily sorry O my God O God into Your hands I commend my spirit I will never more offend You

- Watch! Get down!

That was a voice close to him. Then there were more voices and an explosion louder than all the others and sulphurous smoke that stung his eyes and closed his throat.

- Go around the far side of him!

Myles edged the corner of one eye to a space in the circle of the cross and saw the man going away from him, walking, running, backwards, backwards. Darting figures were closing in on him but the guncracks and the explosions went on. He had his back to a high wire fence beside the motorway and then suddenly he was out of sight. More and more pursuers went with him.

A breeze rippled along Myles' hair and he saw a leaf fly onto a path. It moved weakly from side to side like a lame bird looking for a place to hide.

- Are you all right?

A young priest and an older man stood above him. He was kneeling on the gravel of Eva's grave.

- You weren't hit, were you? asked the priest. His face was elongated on one side, his chin like a wart hanging loose.

- No. I'm okay.

Someone said - Could you come quick, Father?

The priest and the older man went away. Myles rose slowly and rubbed the tears from his eyes. He put his hand on the headstone. It was cold and smooth and comforting. He went to the back of the cross. There were two large dents below the circle of it and spidery lines emanating from them.

He heard the voice of Gerry Adams. The words wafted across the graves.

- What now of all the promises from career politicians, from place-seekers and from partisan and shoneen church leaders?

A grey minibus sped along the cemetery road that led from Milltown's open gates to the Republican plot. Myles flinched and gripped an arm of the cross. The minibus stopped suddenly and a group of men lifted someone slowly, carefully to the space inside. Adams's voice rose, loud and insistent.

- We beg, and I mean beg, the British people to leave us in peace. We do not deserve the suffering that their governments have inflicted upon us.

The drone of the helicopter behind him came closer. He looked and saw it descending slowly towards the M1, then pausing, then rising, then hovering, like a black bug preparing to pounce. The noise of it filled his head till he could hear nothing else and the minutes grew longer and louder and, finally, all thought stopped.

- **What does this mean?**

- **What does what mean?**

- **Am I dead? Are you finished with me?**

- **You're not dead.**

- **So what do you mean by all thought stopped?**

- **Let the reader decide what that means. It's not for you to worry about. You're not dead anyway. I can tell you that for a fact.**

- **Why did you spare me?**

- **Respect. Respect for the dead.**

- **That doesn't make sense.**

- **Yes it does. The shooting and bombing in Milltown cemetery actually happened. I suppose you couldn't have known that. You probably thought it was made up, just like you. Three young men were shot dead by the gunman when they were chasing him. I'm not going to diminish what they** did and the lives they saved by having a fictional character killed as well.

- I see. And what about ....what about ....

- What about what?

- What about ... my little accident?

- No big deal. You're alive, aren't you?

- It isn't exactly dignified, is it?

- And?

- I hope you're not going to be describing my ... my ablutions.

- Ablutions. God, I'm trying to remember the last time I heard that word. You mean cleaning yourself, don't you?

- Yes.

- No. I won't be touching on that.

- Best left to the imagination?

- Best scrubbed from the imagination. Maybe thought about fleetingly but no more than that.

- So. I live on.

- That's right. Now, if you'll excuse me, I have some packing to do.

- Oh?

- Yes. My wife and I are going on holiday.

- Where, if you don't mind my asking?

- Blackpool. She has a sister living in Blackpool.

- How long will you be away for?

- Three weeks.

- That's a long time.

- Very long.

- Will you be doing any writing while you're there?

- No. Unfortunately not. But I'll be thinking about you.
- Oh good.
- I'll be working out whether I've any further use for you.
- Oh.
- Don't let it get you down too much. You've had a fair run. Anyway, I haven't finally decided yet.
- So I sit here for three weeks in a state of ... suspended animation, I suppose you'd call it?
- How about suspended melancholy? Or frozen depression? Or cryogenic sadness?
- Yes. Those are good. I like those.
- Don't try to flatter me.
- Okay. They're crap then.
- That's better. That's my Myles.

Myles' only audience was Maurice McHale.
- You probably saw more than I did, he said to Maurice. - I'd my face pressed against a gravestone most of the time.
- You couldn't see that much on the TV either, said Maurice. - The picture was jerkin about a good lot.
- He shot at me, you know.
- Right enough? said Maurice. - Fuck. I wuda shat meself if somebody'd shot at me. Fuck.
He took off his cloth cap and leaned back to look up at the television set. He swept his hand across some straggling wisps of hair and rocked a little on his stool.

- That Daffy Duck's somethin, he said. - You should watch it.

Myles went behind the bar and through to the lounge. He came back after a minute.

- Pat! he shouted. - Pat!

Maurice gave a loud laugh.

- God, that boy's some character, he said.

He turned to Myles.

- Pat'll be back in a minute. I'm not sure where it was he said he was goin.

A bucket clattered on tiles and Pat came out from the toilet shaking his hands dry.

- It's disgustin, he said. - There's grown men in this town that's still not housetrained. Oh hello, Myles. I'm supposed to be runnin a bar here and what am I? I'm a charwoman and a lavatory cleaner and a....

As his thoughts stalled he moved in behind the bar, snapping away at his fingers.

- You know what I am too? What do you call it when you have to listen to ones tellin you their troubles and they're expectin you to give them all the answers?

- A priest? suggested Maurice.

- I'm not astin you, said Pat, rubbing his hands on a dish towel. - I'm astin Myles here. Myles, what d'you call that person?

- A shrink?

- That's it. The very one, said Pat. - This boy from Shantalla came in today, you know your man John Doherty works in the bookies, and Jesus, you wanted to hear him.

87

You'd think nobody ivir had any bothers only him. Fit to be tied so he was.

- Jung men like that freuden me, said Myles.
- What d'you mean? What d'you mean freuden?
- Aw, you'd need to be from Dublin to get it, said Myles.
- I'll let that pass, said Pat. - The usual?
- Make it a double. Give it to me now, would you.
- Right. Double Jameson on the double.

Pat stopped suddenly, holding the empty glass in the air. He stared at Myles.

- Hey, somebody was sayin you wur up in Belfast today. Jesus, what a scene!
- He was nearly killed, said Maurice. - Yer man Rambo nearly killed him.
- Right enough? said Pat.
- Get me that drink for Christ's sake! shouted Myles.
- Sorry, said Pat.

He got the whiskey in a hurry and handed it across the bar.

- Yeah, I was there, said Myles. He put the trembling glass to his mouth.
- Take it easy, man, said Pat. - That's not water you're drinkin.

Nobody spoke for a couple of minutes. The cartoon ended in a rush of trumpets. Myles placed the drained glass on the bartop.

- Give us another, he said.
- Right. Up and comin.
- I heard on the car radio there's two dead, said Myles.

Pat put the whiskey quickly beside the empty glass.

- Three, he said. - Three dead and sixty or so injured. Jesus, that must have been some scene.

- You were askin me was I shot at, said Myles. - I was, me and a whole lot of other people.

He sipped at his drink.

- Tell me, is Conn comin in tonight, do you know? he asked.

- I thought he might be savin himself for Paddy's night, said Pat, - but seein, seein with all that happenin in Belfast, I'd say he might just land in here sometime.

- You reckon?

- Aw aye. Does he know you wur up at the funerals?

- He does.

- Well then, there you are. He'll be in all right.

He came out from behind the bar and sat on the stool next to Myles.

- Are you all right for drink there, Maurice? he asked.

- Aye, this'll do me, said Maurice. - Unless you're goin to stand me one.

Pat put his head close to Myles' ear. His breath smelled like a saved-up fart.

- Danny got a bad touch last night, he whispered. - Did you hear?

- What do you mean?

- Did you not hear? The Provos. They kneecapped him.

Myles fist whitened on his glass.

- They took him for somebody else, whispered Pat. - They went to the wrong house. They were lookin for somebody that did some violent crime and they went to the wrong fucken house.

- How is he? said Myles.

- Not too good. Alan Kelly was over seein him in the hospital today. They've got him very heavily sedated, Alan says. It seems he might be losin the leg.

- Jesus Christ.

- They wur waitin for him when he got back from here last night. He was in the same taxi as you, wasn't he?

- Yeah, he was.

- Well, they wur in the house waitin for him. They took him out in front of his niece and three wains. Five big brave bastards with masks and guns. They took him out to his back garden and four of them held him down and the other one did the business.

Myles stared through the Guinness mirror for a few moments at his own hunched image. Then he lowered his eyes.

- What about the wains? he asked.

- How d'you mean?

- I mean....

Tears were tugging at his eyes. What was this? It had been a bad day, that was it.

- How d'you mean? repeated Pat.

- I mean who's takin care of them?

- Danny's sister has them. Elaine. She lives over the Lecky Road. Not far from you, actually.

He moved his face closer. The warm foul odour made a rising wave swell in Myles' stomach.

90

- The wee niece fainted and it seems the wains wur in hysterics, said Pat. - They wur dancin round him in the garden screamin till a neighbour woman came along. He could have bled to death so he could.

Pat sniffed hard and rubbed the palm of his hand back and forward across his mouth.

- But the active service unit returned safely to base, he said. - The bastards. Another good night's work for the Ra.

I wish he would go away. How can somebody smell like that and not know? What about his wife? Has she sinus trouble?

- What's that you're sayin about the Ra? asked Maurice.

- Nothin at all, said Pat. - It's not important, Maurice.

He leaned into Myles' face.

- Three, five and seven. That's the ages of them, he said. - Steps of stairs.

- What about yous? said Conn. - You all right Myles?

- Christ you gave me a shock, said Pat. - You must have crept in. Turn that TV down, Maurice. Here, give us the remote.

He stepped off the stool.

- You wouldn't get me and Myles a drink there, would you, Pat? said Conn.

- Sure thing. You can keep an eye on me tonight, Conn. I got distracted last night, if you remember.

- Aye, right, said Conn. - How'd you manage, Myles?

- I wasn't hurt, if that's what you mean.

- Did you hear about Danny? said Pat.

- I did. It's a disgrace.

- Pat was sayin he might lose the leg, said Myles.

- Is that right? said Conn. - Is that right, Pat?

- So Alan Kelly was tellin me, said Pat. - Alan was over seein him.

Myles and Conn went to their corner table.

- Hey Myles, where are you away? shouted Maurice.

- I'm not goin far.

- What's a man like you doin riskin your life with that crowd up in Belfast anyway? Maurice went on. - You could be travellin round the world, an edumicated man like you.

- Sure you know Myles can't travel after the kickin he got, whispered Pat.

- The world's your oxter, shouted Maurice. - Isn't that what they say?

- Oyster, said Pat.

- What?

- It's oyster, Maurice. The world's your oyster. That's what the sayin is.

- How could the world be your oyster? said Maurice. - Sure that's stupid.

Pat brought the whiskey to Myles.

- Thanks, Pat.

Myles turned to Conn.

- The sooner this country's sorted out the better, he said.

- What about the children? asked Conn. - There's three of them, aren't there?

- There are, said Myles. - Danny's sister's takin care of them.

- I meant to go out to the hospital this evenin, said Conn, - but I couldn't make it.

- I'll call for you tomorrow about seven and we'll go and see him, said Myles. - How does that sound?

- Right, said Conn. - That's great.

He looked up at the bar. His Guinness was sitting waiting and Pat was nowhere to be seen. He went over and carried the foaming drink back to the table.

- Tell us about what happened today, he said. - I saw the news.

- I don't know that much, answered Myles. - Would you believe it? From I left Derry till I got back the only person I spoke to was the man at the petrol station. And a priest.

- A priest! You're jokin.

- Naw I'm not. I was crouched down on a grave and he came over and asked me if I'd been shot.

- Jesus.

- There were people fallin all over the place and lyin flat and I didn't know if they'd been hit or if they were tryin to save themselves.

- There were three killed, you know, said Conn.

- Pat told me.

- One of them was a Provo.

- Oh?

- Unarmed. A fella called Kevin Brady. And the killer was arrested. You know about that?

- Yeah. I heard on the car radio. I heard the cops didn't arrive till the crowd of young fellas had got hold of him.

- It stinks, said Conn.

Myles felt the anger rising in his chest but now it was an anger free of fear, seventy miles away from the shock of being there. He tilted his glass and looked at the level of whiskey in it, then slowly drank what was left. There was silence in the bar except for a near inaudible documentary showing on television. Soft stained-glass lights lay on Maurice's shoulders as he perched on his stool, eyes fixed on the screen. Myles got up and went to the toilet. Maurice heard the door click shut and swung round.

- Christ. Look at that there, he said.

Conn looked at the TV. A line of severed heads sat in a neat row on a stone ditch beside a farmhouse. One of the heads had a partly bloodied priest's collar fitted below the chin.

- What's that in their mouths? asked Conn.

- That's balls, said Maurice.

- What! You're not serious.

- That's fucken balls. I'm tellin you. I heard the man sayin.

- My God.

- I heard him sayin there a minute ago. Aren't testicles balls?

- They are.

- Well, that's what he said. I'm tellin you. He said they stuffed their testicles in their mouths. I heard it. Myles, look at that. Look at the TV till you see.

Myles stood at the toilet door, looking up at the screen.

- What? he said.

- Fuck, it's away.

- Don't be sayin, Maurice, said Conn. - He won't thank you for tellin him.

Maurice put his hands across his lips.

94

- What is it, anyway? asked Myles.

- You don't want to hear about it, said Conn.

- What?

- Atrocities in El Salvador.

- Aw Jesus, said Myles. - The old US of A still shittin on other people's doorsteps. Naw, I don't want to hear.

He went to the bar.

- Pat! he shouted. - Where are you hidin?

A voice echoed from the lounge.

- Comin!

- What are you doin in there? This isn't a cleanin service you're runnin. I need a drink.

Pat arrived a little breathlessly.

- My God, man, he said. - Can you not wait a minute?

- I cannot. Give us the same again.

- Don't bother a Guinness for me yet, called Conn.

Myles took a sip from the whiskey on his way to the table. He sighed as he sat down.

- I nearly got it up there today, Conn, he said. - I'm very lucky to be sittin here.

- Jesus, Myles. You should never have gone.

- I wasn't along with the rest of the mourners. I was down at another grave away a bit from the Republican plot and suddenly this boy with the beard appeared out of nowhere and started chuckin grenades and shootin.

- How near were you to him?

- I don't know. From here to the lounge. He didn't see me at the start because I was hidin behind a gravestone but then he spotted me and shot at me. Two bullets hit the gravestone.

- Jesus Christ.

- Then he started comin towards me and I thought I was finished. That's when some of the people turned on him and tried to surround him. Those young fellas didn't know it but they saved my life.

Neither of them spoke for a minute. A dog barked outside and a motorbike revved louder and louder and then went silent. Pat and Maurice were gazing up at the television. President Reagan stood before the press corps, all twinkly eyes and sideways grin.

- I prayed, you know, said Myles.

- Okay, said Conn. - I can understand that. Old habits die hard.

- Naw. The buttermilk came through the brochan, Conn. At the back of it I'm still a superstitious shit-scared Catholic.

- I don't know about that.

- I know, said Myles. - Here's me, the confirmed humanist ridiculin the idea of God and there's what I turn round and do.

- I thought you said to me one time you were agnostic.

- I probably did. That would have been before my conversion.

Myles half laughed and drank some more from his whiskey.

- That feels better, he said. - I feel the buzz. I'm goin to get blutthered tonight.

- I wouldn't blame you.

- You go into the chapel any quiet time of the day, said Myles,

96

- and I'll bet you it's still the same. The ones you see makin visits to the Blessed Sacrament are nearly all old. I envy them. I used to think that when I got older and the time got shorter I'd want to keep in with God too. But it's turned out the opposite. The older I get the more cynical I get.

He paused. His breath came in short bursts now. Conn looked sideways at him. There was a high colour across his forehead and a grey pallor over the rest of his face.

- And then there's all these educated ones, he continued, - that go along with the mumbo jumbo when their brains tell them the opposite.

- That's me, said Conn. - I'm one of them. I practise just in case. Every time I go to mass and Holy Communion I'm payin the next premium of the insurance policy. I keep hopin it's not a scam.

- Yeah, but you get comfort sometimes, don't you?

- Sometimes. But mostly it's like shakin your fist in the dark. I'm nearly as cynical as you, Myles, only I don't have it in me to make the break.

- Aw, you'd have the balls all right. I'd say there's still a bit of belief there.

Myles got up and went to the bar. He came back after a minute with another Jameson.

- Pat will have a Guinness over shortly, he said.

- Guaranteed before the end of the week.

Small groups of people were coming into the bar in something of a rush now as if a red light outside had suddenly turned to green. The door swung open and closed again and again, ushering in draughts of cold evening air.

- Sometimes I say to myself, said Myles, - How the fuck did I get caught up in all this?

- How do you mean?

- Life, I'm talkin about. It's like the graffiti they had on a wall in Belfast years ago. You remember? *Is there life before death?*

- Aye, I remember that, said Conn.

- Nobody asked me to join up, went on Myles. - I was thrown in and I just had to lump it. Same with you. Shanghaied. Tell us this. Who's in charge? Who do you write to to complain?

He raised his glass towards Conn for a moment and said - I hope you didn't take offence there when I was sayin about educated ones.

- Not at all. I wonder myself sometimes if I'm right in the head.

- I was at mass last Christmas, said Myles. - I'm hardly one to be talkin.

- Were you, right enough?

- Yeah. It was a funny thing. My sister Anne was over from Blackpool and I brought her to midnight mass in Saint Eugene's. I actually got quite emotional.

- Really?

- Yeah. When the choir sang *Silent Night* I felt the old tingles. You know the old tingles? And then the junior choir sang *All in a Stable*.

- Time for the tissues?

- Near enough. It was like childhood comin back. The excitement and the security and all the rest. It was as if I'd

98

passed out of that world but now I was back in it.

- It can get to you all right, said Conn.

The Drunken Dog had filled earlier than usual. A crowd of men and women were singing quietly among themselves. As they neared the end of the song there was something of a hush in the rest of the bar.

I love you as I've never loved before
Since first I met you on the village green.
Come to me ere my dream of love is o'er.
I love you as I loved you
When you were sweet,
When you were sweet sixteen

The last words were followed by applause, mostly from the singers themselves. Somebody called out - Myles, give us Boolavogue, would ye.

- I will not, retorted Myles.

- Come on, what about it? somebody else called.

- I'll never sing a rebel song again, shouted Myles. - What we need in this country is less singin and more doin.

- There's Michael, said a woman. - Michael, give us *A Nation Once Again*.

The tall darkhaired young man was standing on his own at the end of the bar next to the side exit. He threw back the rest of his drink and reached for the door handle.

- Naw, listen, he said. - I'm headin out.

- You are not, insisted Pat and he set a pint of Harp in front of him. - That's on me. Give us a song now. But don't be singin that one or the peelers'll be in on top of us.

- What about *The Foggy Dew*? somebody shouted.

Michael shook his head. Then he took a sip from his glass and started. The slow sad air that he sang was one that neither Myles nor Conn had heard before and the words were in a Gaelic dialect they couldn't understand. At first the notes came faltering but by the third line the soft tenor tones were strong and sure. Twice there were unexpected lilts and trills that took the listeners by surprise. The room fell silent at the sudden swoops in the music and before the end not even the tinkle of a glass disturbed the song. When he finished there was loud applause and several people called for more. But Michael smiled and said no. He lifted his drink and came over to Myles and Conn.

- That was lovely, Michael, said Conn.

- I never heard you singin as well, said Myles, his eyes shining.

- Thanks, said Michael. - Yous don't mind me sittin here a minute, do yous? There was somethin I wanted to ask you, Myles.

Conn reached sideways for a low stool and put it beside the table. - Here. Sit down there.

- It's a pleasure and a privilege, said Myles. - What did you want to ask me?

Michael sat on the stool and edged it closer to the table. - I heard tonight that the cardinals aren't goin to have the pastoral read out at the masses tomorrow.

- I didn't know that, said Myles. - But I'm not surprised.

- What I can't understand, continued Michael, - is this. How do the killins in Milltown change anythin? I mean, that's why they've stopped the pastoral, isn't it?

- Must be, said Conn.

Michael leaned forward, elbows on the table. - There's people bein killed every day. Why should they put off the pastoral just because three more die?

Myles spoke gently. - Michael, the four churchmen knew they wouldn't get away with it after what happened today.

Michael opened his mouth to say something and then stopped.

- The pastoral's not true, said Myles. - It's a political statement and it's not true. It's basically tellin Catholics to say, "Hey, big Brit, I know you're goin to keep puttin the boot in but I still want to be your friend."

- That can't be, objected Michael. - Cardinal O'Fiaich's a good man. Sure didn't the British government try and stop him bein made cardinal because he was too much of an Irishman?

- They did, agreed Myles. - and he still is. But pressure can make people do things sometimes.

- Hey, hold on, said Conn. - I think we'd better quieten down. We're gettin dirty looks.

Molly Doherty had taken the floor and was somewhere in the third verse of a comeallye to a background of clenched murmurs. Myles had his mouth shut tightly now but his nose made a sound like the hiss of air from a flattening tyre. Molly finally sat down and relieved applause rippled round the room.

- When our day comes, said Myles, - and I'm minister for culture and the arts in the new Ireland, the first bill I'm goin to introduce in the dollhouse is goin to be the transportation bill.

- The dollhouse? asked Michael. - You mean the Dáil?

- I mean the dollhouse, Myles said firmly.

- What has transport got to do with culture? said Conn.

Myles wiped his mouth with the back of his hand. - Not transport. Transport*ation*. When the bill becomes law it'll mean that anybody of sound mind who's found to have sung in excess of eleven verses of an Irish comeallye to an audience of one or more persons will be deported forthwith to Australia.

- Is that not a bit harsh? asked Michael, smiling.

- Not at all, responded Myles. - Australians deserve all they get. Remember, this is the country that gave us *Waltzing Matilda*.

- That's right, said Conn. - And what about the accent?

- Exactly! said Myles. - For that alone they deserve it.

Michael threw back his head and laughed. - You're a goodun, Myles.

He stood up. - Listen, I have to go. I'm on nights this week. But I enjoyed the crack.

- You're leavin half your pint, said Conn. - Why don't you finish it before you go?

- Naw, I only came in for the one, answered Michael. - I'm just goin to slip out here. I'll see yous.

- Take it easy, said Myles.

- Right. See you, Michael, said Conn.

When Michael had gone Myles signalled for a drink.

- Is that the fingers you're givin me or is it a double you're lookin for? shouted Pat.

- Both, Myles shouted back. - And get a Guinness movin too.

102

He turned to Conn. - Great lad, Michael.

- Aye, said Conn, - and one of the best tenors in Derry. He could go places if he got that voice of his trained.

Myles lifted a beer mat from the table. - What age would you say he was?

- I know what age he is. He's twenty-seven.

- Twenty-seven, said Myles. - That's about the age my boy would have been.

- Right enough?

- Yeah. I told you before, didn't I?

- You talked about it one time, said Conn.

Myles folded the beer mat in two. - He was stillborn. I was just thinkin on the way back from Belfast. I'll not be leavin anybody behind. I'll disappear without trace. That's what I was thinkin.

- I don't know about that, said Conn. - You taught a lot of boys in your time. Plenty of them will remember you. I'll remember you. Half of Derry will remember you.

- It's not the same, said Myles.

He began breaking tiny pieces from the beer mat. - I had the child with a girl in London. Eva. She was from Andersonstown actually but she was livin over there at the time. Chalk Farm.

- Aye?

- She's dead now. She died young. Did I tell you that?

Before Conn could answer Myles coughed loudly and gave a half laugh.

- She was a great girl, he said. - I was over for a few weeks bummin round the place before I started teachin here and

103

she let me stay with her in this bedsit she had.

- You charmed her.

- I did. I charmed her. She knew I was a chancer but she didn't mind.

- When was that? What year?

- The summer of nineteen sixty. It was great.

He didn't speak for a minute and then he laughed again. - I don't think I told you this. She was a typist in the Catholic Herald and one day I met her comin out of work and she'd two copies of that day's paper with her and she'd got new headlines put on the front page of just these two copies. Big banner headlines.

- Right?

- CASTRO TELLS POPE TO FUCK OFF. Well, the two of us sat together on the tube holdin the papers up in front of us as if we were readin the back pages. You wanted to see the looks on the faces opposite.

Conn smiled broadly. - That must have been somethin.

- Pure joy. And wait till you hear. The stop before Chalk Farm these two nuns got on and sat facin us. I mean, we couldn't believe our luck. How often do you see a nun on the London underground?

One of the drinkers came over and left a large Jameson in front of Myles.

- Regards from Pat, he said.

- Thanks, Liam, said Myles. - You're a gentleman.

He sipped the last of his old whiskey and chuckled quietly to himself.

- You got married in sixty-four, didn't you? asked Conn.

- That's right. Susan. Susan couldn't have children.

- That's a pity.

- Yeah. She was as dry as a bone and as frigid as fuck.

Myles gathered all the crumbles from the beer mat and swept them into an ashtray with the side of his hand. - Do you know this, Conn? I married that girl so's I could get to bed with her. Would you believe it? I mean, that's how it was. The swingin Sixties. Big joke. I was a randy wee Catholic and she was a real woman of the world. You remember the ones? Loud, equal and those hard blue jeans. Fuck.

- I remember them, said Conn. - Like metal.

- Yeah, but I was waitin for what was underneath. And I waited and waited. Christ I waited. She had me out of my mind so she did. But do you know somethin? She was the only person I'd ever met that had actually read *Ulysses*. Apart from myself.

He turned to Conn and looked at him frankly. - Tell me the honest truth if you don't mind me askin. Have you ever read it?

- I read about it.

- Naw but have you ever read it? The fucken book, I'm talkin about.

- Forty or fifty pages of it.

- That's what I mean, said Myles. - In nineteen sixty-four, the time I'm tellin you about, the only people in the world who'd ever read the whole book, apart from me and Susan, were eight American eggheads and some eccentric from Carlow.

- And Joyce himself, of course.

- I doubt it.

- What d'you mean? Sure he's the one that wrote it.

- Different thing, insisted Myles. - It took him seven years to write it and by the time he was finished he was nearly ready for the straitjacket. Do you seriously think he was goin to squander what was left of his sanity by actually *readin* the thing?

- I see what you mean.

- Naw. He was plannin *Finnegans Wake* and he reckoned he'd have to stay sane for that. Though I'm not sure he did. Did you ever read *that*?

- First two lines, said Conn.

- Not bad. Probably more than some of the boys that wrote about it.

Myles laughed. - Anyway, I was tellin you about Susan. I used to question her about *Ulysses*, you know, pretendin I was just discussin it. She'd read it all right. And she'd this Paris edition of *The Ginger Man* that was published as a pornographic book. You've read it, haven't you?

- I have. Every word.

- Do you remember the oral sex scenes? Well, she used to go on about them as if she was talkin about chicken drumsticks or somethin. But she never let me past the tight squeeze and she always seemed to be holdin me off, you know, savin herself for the big surrender and all. Jesus Christ, Conn, I was like somethin shot out of a cannon the first night. Zoom boom. Except the castle wall held firm, nuptials and all.

- Impregnable?

- She might as well have been wearin a fucken drawbridge. You know, when it's up the ways. By the time I got in two weeks later I was nearly dead. What the fuck are you laughin at?

- Sorry, said Conn. - But it's funny.

- It's not really, you know, retorted Myles with sudden intensity. He went quiet for a minute then, shaking his head several times and whispering something to himself that Conn couldn't hear properly.

- Sorry, you've no what?

- I've no respect, Myles mumbled. He paused and then said it again, clearly. He went on:

- Susan was what they used to call a good-livin girl. You remember what that meant, don't you? It meant she was scared to death of her own instincts.

- Terrible, said Conn.

Myles scowled. - You want to read what Joyce said about that kind of thing. Did I ever tell you what he said? "There's no heresy as abhorrent to the Catholic Church as the human body." That was it.

- Sure you remember what they did to me, said Conn quietly.

- Right, said Myles, eyes staring, head nodding hard. - You had to go in for a while, didn't you?

- I was in more than four months. I thought I was never goin to get out. They kept givin me the electric shocks. You know, the ECT. It's like gettin your brain fried so it is.

- What age were you? Eighteen?

- Seventeen.

- It's criminal, said Myles. - The Church gives you the fire and brimstone treatment from you're seven and then when you're seventeen the Health Service takes over.

- What is it the Jesuits say? said Conn.

- How in under fuck has the Catholic Church survived for two thousand years is what I'd like to know, muttered Myles.

- Naw, I don't think they say that, said Conn, laughing.

- Shhh, whispered Myles. - Look. Behold. There's Pat comin with your drink. That's the first time he's ever been known to pull a Guinness on schedule without havin his wife held hostage.

- Thanks, Pat, said Conn.

- Don't mention it son, replied Pat and went back behind the bar.

Conn watched the stout slowly settle. - I shouldn't be takin this one at all, you know. I've the interview on Friday and I want to get myself all bushy-tailed.

Myles put his hand to his forehead. - I forgot. I forgot all about it. Jesus, that's the day after tomorrow.

- Aye. They say they want to get it all sorted out before the Easter holidays.

Myles looked at the ceiling and prayed:

> - Blessed Michael the Archangel,
> Defend us in this New hour of Conflict!
> Scourge of the infidel!
> Prince of the heavenly host!
> The hour is nigh, the Connman cometh!
> For I hear the clatter of his cloven hoof!

Secure the gates of All Saints
Against this Doherty, this straight-kneed wanker!
Awake! Awake! Strengthen the resolve
Of Josie the Falangelist
And Babbie his high priest!
Let them not be Conned, we pray you.
Help them show their grit
Against the shit.
Keep All Saints Catholic!

Conn smiled.

- Tell me this, Corrigan. Whose side are you on anyway?

- I'm on the winner's side. Always flexible. Fluid as fuck. What I say is, best of luck to the winner. I learned that from the Church, you know.

- Right enough?

- Yeah. I asked you a stupid question there now. Remember I asked you how they'd survived for two thousand years?

- I remember.

- Well, here's how they survived. They're nimble, you see. One day they're condemnin political movements from the pulpit and the next day they're invitin them to open schools.

Conn laughed. - So should I sell my soul on Friday?

- Naw, you don't have to sell it. Just pawn it and then redeem it whenever they give you the job. Simple.

- Fairytale stuff, said Conn. - But you know what I'd love to do?

- What?

- I'd love to tell them what I really think. That'd be somethin.

The bar was uproarious now. Around Myles and Conn men and women were shouting into each other's ears, blaring and braying like people demented. Swirls of cigarette smoke rose to a cloud that floated between the ceiling and the drinkers' heads and the sound of punk thudded through the archway from the lounge.

Conn stood up. - I must go. You make sure and get a taxi.

- I'll do that, said Myles. - Though I wouldn't mind wanderin through the town a bit and lookin up at the stars.

- A taxi! D'you hear me? said Conn. - Will I order it now for a certain time?

- Not at all. I'm only jokin. I've had enough excitement for one day. Hey, listen. I take it you're goin to have a quiet Paddy's day?

- I am, said Conn. - I'll be stewin up on all the latest education guidelines.

- Hold on. Amn't I callin for you tomorrow evenin to go and see Danny?

- That's right. I forgot, said Conn.

He moved towards the door.

- Listen! shouted Myles. - Don't you be chasin after all these new education ideas now. Remember what the old Christian Brother used to say: "They're like buses and women. There's always goin to be another one round the corner."

- Right, Conn shouted back, not hearing him.

Myles sat tingling with contentment. The whiskey and the company had warmed him and he felt flushed and comfortable. The picture of his flat clicked in his head for a moment and straightaway he put away the thought of going back to it. Better to be alone here among the roaring drinkers and the pumping music. He picked up an evening newspaper from the windowsill behind him and held it upright between himself and the noise. His mind flitted through the pages, sipping and spitting as it went. Christians and Muslims at each other's throats in Azerbaijan. The Sharpeville Six sentenced to death in South Africa for killing the man they called a quisling. Raped Pakistani girl swallows pesticide to save the family honour. Three mourners lie dead in Belfast. Three children cry in their beds in Derry. Chinese authorities torture Tibetans in Lhasa. Western lifestyle is the work of Satan, says Islamic cleric. Salvadoreans mark eighth anniversary of the assassination of Archbishop Romero by US-backed junta. An earthquake, a flood, a story of kiss and tell, the homeless eyes of a Sudanese toddler, mouth agape, thin cling of phlegm between dry lips.

He left down the paper and looked at his watch. There'd be time for another double before last orders. The difference between the half lucid and the near oblivion. To do or not to do. He lifted his glass and studied it. It glowed amber and black. There was enough. He drank from it and its friendly kick caught him unawares for a moment. Three men argued about a dog, nobbled or not he couldn't tell. A shimmering girl in a smoky-blue dress swayed against a table and a full pint glass toppled in slow motion. Myles saw this from the beginning and told no one. Somebody howled in his ear at somebody else. A secret thought came and the rising volume kept it private and uninterrupted. He would have been a good

111

father. Michael would have been a good son. It could have been different.

There was a roll of drums from the lounge and then the words and music of the weekly finale. Gunga Din Doherty's voice carried powerfully into the bar and the drinkers around Myles joined in.

> *Then sings my soul, my Saviour God, to Thee,*
> *How great Thou art, how great Thou art!*

The mood seemed to flip in an instant and the barroom was godhappy and defiant. Some people stood with one clenched fist in the air and others had two free hands raised, palms open. While all around him stood in tribute Myles sat quietly righteous and nursed a new secret thought. Islam's extremists are on the margins, Christianity's are in the mainstream. There's Jip Mullholland. When was it? Twenty-three years ago next June he near enough castrated me in a friendly match, kicked me so hard I was four days in hospital. He doesn't play football anymore but he still kicks, the bastard. And there he is singing his heart out, eyes gentle as Jesus. And Nancy Kelly, a great girl. What the hell's she doing gone like that, saluting a deity she doesn't know the first thing about? And Micky Macker, here with his fancy woman and his wife in hospital waiting to give birth. But maybe I've got it wrong. Maybe the baby's born and all's well and Micky's taken the dolly bird out to celebrate. How quick we are to judge.

The song finished and fervour spent, the drinkers settled

back to screaming into each other's faces. Myles turned his head a little, intending to speak to a boy now sitting in Conn's place. He was sixteen or seventeen and his eyes were glazed or possibly crossed. But the girl on his lap seemed sober. So Myles spoke to her instead. - Faith is believin what you know isn't true, he explained. - That's what people don't realize.

She stared at him with her mouth wide open and he couldn't tell if she was outraged or just stupid. Someone to his left had started to sing and the room was quietening.

Twas down by the glenside I met an old woman
A-pluckin young nettles nor yet saw me comin.
I listened awhile to the song she was hummin:
"Glory O, glory O to the bold Fenian men".

It was being sung by a tousle-haired teenager and he was off-key. But his heart was in the song and Myles was pleased at that. It was the one more than any other that he remembered from his childhood. So he was surprised when he leaned forward to say to a man just in front of him - What we need in this country is less singin and more doin.

The man shushed him and when the song was over and people were cheering he stooped close to Myles and whispered - That fella's a Provo. You'd need to watch your mouth, friend.

Myles nodded. After a minute he rose and made his way carefully to the bar. He said to Pat - You wouldn't ring a taxi for me, would you?

Pat said - Thur's an empty one outside. If you go now quick you might be lucky.

113

While the taxi waited in the checkpoint queue Myles turned to the river and thought of James Joyce and John Jameson. Joyce said one time that Jameson's whiskey got its tang from the muddy unfiltered waters of the Liffey. Maybe this was a joke. If it was then Myles didn't understand it.

He looked across the dark width of the Foyle to where it met the Waterside. Headlights flowing down a brae beyond the opposite bank left brightness guttering in the river. Was it a trick of the heaving tide or was someone in the water? He wound down the window. Yes, it looked like someone. Nobody he knew, though. The driver was a surly sort of boyo, one of these uncommunicative bastards you get sometimes. So Myles decided not to tell him. Let him read it in tomorrow's evening paper. Whoever it was, they were waving and drowning. Yes, that's what they were doing, drowning away, waving goodbye. Whoever it was, they wanted to die. Well, good luck. But you realize you're never going to get to the other side, don't you? I just thought I'd tell you that. Maybe you knew already. In which case, forget I spoke.

I'm tired of everything. I think I'll sleep till the afternoon. Conn says, he says, what does he say? He says we're like the fish and the fowl. He says if we lie too long we go bad. Conn's right. I need to change direction. Starting the morning after tomorrow.

- There's a woman in Camden Town, she said, - and she's supposed to be very good. You used to hear about the ones with the wire coat hangers. She's not like that. I've it all checked.

114

- You'll know when it's over, she promised. - I'll ring you from the phone on the stairs. Sure it's right outside my door. Don't fuss now. If I haven't called by a quarter past five you'll know to ring the hospital.

She put on the swanky accent. - Is this The Drunken Dog? Could I please speak to Myles Corrigan? It's a real funny name for a pub. Where did they get a name like that? I can't wait to hear your voice.

Willie Ned started on the phone at ten to five. Between that and twenty to six he must have spent three pounds. And him after losing big money too.

*- I missed out on the treble and two other doubles by **that** much. I should have backed a draw like the ref did. If Chelsea had won I was gettin a hundred and thirty odd. One offside goal and I'm more than a hundred down. Fucken right. Ye can't beat them. What? Too fucken right. A treble like that only comes up once in a whatd'yecallit.*

I was civil. I told him over and over again and then when I took the phone out of his hand he got me by the throat. How is it ugly people are more violent than the rest of us? That face pitted with pockmarks. I won't forget it. And then he was hardly out the door when the barman told me.

- There's somethin up with that phone today, son. It's not takin incomin calls.

The phone on the stairs rang and rang but the hospital one answered right away. Better to be in trouble and alive than in the clear and dead.

The two of them died on the bed I fucked her on. I fucked her all right. She asked for more and I gave it with pleasure. I was good. I was the lover she dreamed of. Oh yes. Except it was over and I wasn't coming back and I never told her. What was it? She wanted me too much? Damaged goods? Respectable teacher washes his hands? I didn't love her? Yes, I didn't love her. Only I did and I didn't know. And if there had been an old head on my shoulders? Then what would I have been? A frankenstein freak. That's right. I did the honest thing.

A faint foul smell touched his nostrils. He wound up the window and then jumped in fright when he heard the Geordie lilt from the other side of him.

- Where are you headed, sir?

Myles turned to look at the blackened face.

- Bottom of Bishop Street, he said.

- Right. Go ahead, said the soldier.

The taxi moved on.

Father Timothy Babb looked intently across at Conn.

- That was most interesting, Mister Doherty, he said.

- Now I think we'd all be very grateful to hear your views on the EMU initiative.

He smiled thinly. - And we'd appreciate it if you would speak briefly this time.

Conn gave a little cough. He was aware that the votes of five or possibly six of the ten people opposite were still in the balance. The rest wouldn't be voting for him.

- Well, he said. - I feel that this is something that should be wholeheartedly embraced by all schools of whatever

116

religious persuasion.

Josie Rabbitt's chair shifted impatiently. Conn sensed malice in the glint of his glasses.

- Education for Mutual Understanding, continued Conn, - or EMU as you quite rightly call it, Father, has a very important contribution to make in bringing together Catholic and Protestant children in this divided part of the world. The vast sums of money the British government is devoting to the initiative will bear fruit only if it receives the support of everybody.

From behind frank and friendly eyes Conn considered the priest.

The truth is, of course, that just like the Australian bird of the same name, this venture will run and run but will never take off. You may know, Father, though you probably don't, that the emu is closely related to the ostrich which spends most of its time with its head up its arse. And, to tell you the truth, not being an ornithologist, I was never able to spot the difference between the two.

- I'm delighted with the news that you endorse EMU, said Josie Rabbitt. - Now, would you please tell the board exactly what you have done in the two years it's been operating.

I'm glad you asked me that, Josie. And may I say how much I welcome the open-ended nature of your question. For most of those two years I've been blundering about looking for love. Latterly I've been banging away at Melanie Muldoon from the Creggan Estate. She's only five foot tall but boy, can she hump! It wouldn't be too far off the mark to say that she gives as good as she gets. However, I only have her at the weekends.

Unfortunately I'm being forced to share her with a shitball called Mickey Scanlon from out the Glen. As a consequence of this I find that I've been spending an exhausting amount of my time with Melanie trying to satisfy her needs in an effort to get her to ditch Mickey. Now Melanie is an extremely fit and rather ravenous girl and my efforts have been mostly at the expense of my own pleasure, as I'm sure you can probably imagine, Josie. Interestingly, though, I've discovered that the more I deny myself the more attached to her I've become. And this metaphysical aspect of our affair brings me to the core of your question. Namely, what have I been doing these past two years? At the risk of repeating myself, I've been searching for a sexual relationship that isn't entirely rooted in sex. I've been with four other girls during this time, all of them animals. You wouldn't believe the modern girl. Hump hump hump. And that's all you get. Honestly, I don't know what the world's coming to.

These thoughts, of course, may well be the meanderings of a middle-aged has-been. I don't think I told you this but Melanie's just over half my age. Consequently, it's more than likely that she'll soon come round to the view that, given my age and physical condition and Mickey's relative youth, he'll still be motoring along when I'm running on empty. However, if and when that happens, you can be assured that the search will continue.

- As you may all know, answered Conn, - I've been involved in running sport in this school for not just two but twenty-seven years. During that time the boys of All Saints have met and competed against countless Church of Ireland, Methodist and Presbyterian lads. I've also helped for many years to select and train the Derry and District schools' soccer teams which, of course, are interdenominational. They subsequently meet and mingle with similar teams from all over the Six Counties.

Father Babb emitted a muffled snort and immediately took a fit of coughing. Conn waited for it to subside and then continued. - The boys I was involved with in my early days are now in their mid to late thirties and many of them have told me they've still got fond memories of the excitement and rivalry and camaraderie that came from their association with boys of their own and other religions.

Josie Rabbitt was puffing his cheeks restlessly.

- The last two years, Mr Doherty, he said. - I'm talking about EMU. What involvement have you had in *that*?

- Well, as I've just explained, I've been at the heart of education for mutual understanding during that time and before.

- I think, interjected Father Babb, - that Mister Rabbitt wants to know in what ways you've taken part in this *specific project.*

Conn swallowed some spittles and scrutinised the middle distance.

EMU, as you all know but won't admit, is an artifice dreamed up by Britain to give the impression that they care about Micks and Dicks getting on with each other here. In fact, the Brits created this shambles by colonising the place away back and they've been dividing and ruling us ever since. They want the world to think they're here to stop two savage tribes killing each other when in fact it is they themselves who have promoted

119

the killing. They know that spending millions on sending Catholics and Protestant children away on free trips together improves virtually nothing except their own image. But they don't seem to have caught on yet that the only thing that would really help this part of the world would be for them to declare an intent to clear off and leave us Micks and Dicks to sort out their mess.

- The reality is, said Conn, - that I simply haven't been able to devote any time to the initiative because of my heavy involvement in sport within the school and in interschool and interdistrict competitions. Mister McGrotty has accepted that this is the situation. But, as I've said, my commitment to education for mutual understanding has been as strong these past two years as it was for the previous twenty-five.

Father Babb put a hand to his jaw and said through half closed fingers - I think we have the picture, Mister Doherty.

He looked at his watch and gave a little start.

- Oh! We may be in danger of overrunning our time here, he said. -We don't want to be giving Mister Doherty an unfair advantage now, do we? he added, snapping shut the black file that sat on his knee. The suspicion of a smile creaked across his face and a cold hard hand came down on the cockles of Conn's heart.

- Just one last thing, said the priest, suddenly leaning forward and craning his neck to look out the window. - From where I'm sitting I can see part of the school car park. Tell me, would that be your silver Saab out there, by any chance?

- Yes, answered Conn. - That's mine.

- I was just wondering, continued Father Babb. - Do you never feel a little self-conscious driving a model like that into an area as deprived as this?

- I'm sorry, Father, said Conn. - I don't....

- Yes?

- I'm afraid I don't see the relevance.

- Really? said Father Babb. - Well, it just seems rather....

Blinking bemusedly, he stretched his hand loosely forward, palm upward as if waiting for the right words to land on it.

- ...rather inappropriate to own a status car such as that when you're teaching in All Saints.

- I think that's a matter for me, Father, said Conn.

- Yes, yes, yes, said Father Babb, releasing a wan conciliatory smile. - Of course. You're quite free to—

- Just as your black Audi is a matter for you, continued Conn.

That's it. That's the clincher. The job's mine.

- Yes, yes, said Father Babb. - Thank you for your time, Mister Doherty. Now would you be good enough to ask Miss Givens to come in right away?

- Yes, Father.

The chapel bell tolled and the funeral of Kevin Brady moved slowly away from Saint Agnes's. A piper walked alone in front of the hefted coffin and his lament wavered and then lingered in the soft noon breeze. Tension pressed on the throng that moved along the Andersonstown Road towards Milltown cemetery. Media men on garden walls focused on the unheeding thousands and the murmurs from the people were quieter than their footsteps on the tarmac and quieter still than the throb of the hovering helicopters.

An engine revved somewhere, sudden and grating, and shouts of stewards carried from down the road:

- Stop!

- Veer him off!

- Watch! He's got a gun!

Disbelief and terror came down like the claws of a hammer and for moments the procession stood rigid. A Volkswagen Passat careered up the Andersonstown Road straight at the black taxis hunched in front of the mourners and then jerked screeching onto the footpath. Men and women threw themselves backwards and sideways over fences and low walls. Newsmen raced forward to film what they could. The car trundled hard along the cleared way and then slowed and stopped and shuddered, blocked by a stonefaced clutch of people that materialised and grew before the driver's eyes.

- For Jesus sake reverse! screamed the passenger and fumbled in the glove compartment.

- The other one's got a gun too!

- Get down!

Hoarse roars of anger clashed with cries and moans and the car yelped into reverse. It screamed onto the road again and then quite suddenly it had nowhere more to go for in front of it and behind it black taxis sat massed like giant cockroaches.

The passenger let loose a stream of pleas and a radio voice crackled back at him. The driver stood leaning his backside against the headrest, legs akimbo, upper body protruding through the open window. He held a gun in the air and shouted - Out of the way you bastards!

Three photographers vying for a vantage point sank to the ground like a collapsed tripod as he fired over their heads. The advancing people stopped and then drew back a little but almost immediately surged forward again. The car window slid up and the two men locked the doors and waited, their radio silent.

Father Timothy Babb was exasperated. His sermon had been written and now this. A different subject and the worst one of all too. He paced the carpet of his study again and again, stopping occasionally at the window to stare unseeing at the sweep of car lights in the Bogside below. His legs were heavy like lead but the rest of his body felt open and defenceless. A sharp insistent pulse stabbed at his temples and no matter how many times he tried to pray it away it kept on coming, beating to the rhythm of his heart.

There was no peace, no respite. But for all that, this was something he had to get right. Yet how? Saturday sport had crowded out any detailed account of the attack. And it was too sudden, too immediate. He went back to his desk, sat down and looked at his own scrawled summary of what the cardinal had said on the radio.

Everyone with a human heart will be sickened by the ghoulishness of this crime.

That would have to do. He could work with that. Strong, uncompromising, like the man himself.

A spade by any other name is still a spade.

He had once heard the cardinal say those memorable words. When was it? He couldn't remember. Where would you get a man closer to Christ than Tomas O'Fiaich? Not anywhere, not this side of the grave anyway.

Father Babb gripped the biro and began.

Such savagery, he wrote. *Such evil. Bombarding the car with metal rods and spikes. Beating and dragging two disarmed men into Casement Park, the proud historic arena of the Gaelic Athletic Association, besmirching the name of one of Ireland's foremost patriots, tearing off defenceless men's clothes and then shooting them in the back of the head as if they were rabid dogs. Dear God, what have we come to? Who, I have to ask, who are the rabid ones?*

He flinched a little and drew a line through the last sentence. *I don't want to alienate any of the good people. I have to somehow walk the narrow road between denouncing evil and upsetting the faithful. Those good people are outraged by the stupid lapses of the military and the shenanigans of maverick policemen and so many of them are confused and ambivalent about these IRA murderers. These Republicans, these coarse cruel perpetrators with their harsh town voices and easy slogans. They know nothing of the true values of our country, them with their loud patriotic pretensions. It usedn't to be like this. These same killers used to flock to devotions and confraternities and now they question and challenge the humble priest. They cannot see that the parish is the rock of our civilisation, where all the faithful have their places. Once respect goes, that's when the crumbling begins.*

Father Babb's shoulders sagged and he stared across the room, his eyes unblinking, his mind trying to focus on what he would write. After a few moments he looked back at the words on the sheet. ***Dear God, what have we come to?*** Yes, that's good. That's true. The sweat stood crowded on his forehead and a bead of it fell from his eyebrow on to the page below. Every breath he breathed was broken by the quickened beats from his heart.

What have we come to? We the priests. What a state of affairs when you have to watch every word you say. Why couldn't these so-called patriots stop for a moment and listen to the words of Christ? Render onto Caesar the things that are Caesar's and onto God the things that are God's. Everything was so different before the agitation. There was cruelty and deprivation but people accepted these things with equanimity, with dignity. And yes, with forgiveness. He remembered the packed Church of the Sacred Heart on the day of his ordination. Cardinal Conway, the bishops and the monsignor were there in their robes, yes, but mostly it was the ordinary people of the parishes. He remembered how his mother had glowed, standing with him and the cardinal at the entrance to the magnificent church. He glanced up at the photograph on the mantelpiece. There she was, statuesque and proud. So old now, so frail, her mind gone away. It was she who had sparked his love for the priesthood, his love that grew as he grew and then inflamed his very soul. The walks in the woods above Carndonagh where, each time, they stopped at the mass rock and she told him a little more. The nondescript rock that became the secret sacred altar at the appointed times. The priests that lived like hunted animals, harboured by a brave and destitute people. And always, always, the fear of the turncoat. But you had to try and trust everyone and let the wise and willing detect the dangers.

Each month of May his mother and he would pick wildflowers and lay them on the altar. It was she who had taught him the beautiful words and music that opened his soul then and opened it again now every time he watched the children of All Saints decorating their May altar and listened to their sweet voices.

Bring flowers of the rarest, bring blossoms the fairest,
From gardens and woodlands and hillside and dale.
Our full hearts are swelling, our glad voices telling
The praise of the loveliest flower of the vale.

O Mary we crown thee with blossoms today,
Queen of the angels and queen of the May.
O Mary we crown thee with blossoms today,
Queen of the angels and queen of the May.

I'll go and see her tomorrow after twelve mass, he thought. I'll sleep well and then I'll go and see her. He shook his shoulders and dragged his mind back to the present passing time. It was the politics that depressed him. He'd only ever wanted to be a priest. But the soil and the toil of politics sickened him everywhere he turned. The shining stone of Irish Christianity had been wrenched from the land and there on its underside were the wriggling slimy worms of republicanism. *And their support is growing. More and more of the half-educated and brainwashed are joining their ranks. For what? How many of their band have they buried this week alone? Eight? Nine? Why can they not see that if only they would stop now the security forces would have no excuse for their excesses. And the loyalist revenge killings would stop too.*

But I'm not thinking straight. The oppression and the reprisals are part of the Sinn Féin script. Yes, Adams and McGuinness wring their hands in public and rub them in private. Look at the tens of thousands they can get out to the funerals. It makes you wonder about human nature. Augustine was right. Pelagius was wrong. We were born evil. But you can't say that. I'm a priest and I'm not allowed to tell my people the truth.

He closed his eyes for a while and contemplated the crucified Christ. Then he wrote quickly:

Only by turning to Our Lord Jesus and trying to be like Him can we achieve peace and salvation. Only by offering up our sufferings and praying for that peace can we become truly Christian.

For half an hour he scribbled and highlighted and replaced words and phrases with others. Then he read through what he'd written. He was reading it for a second time when there was a light knock on his study door.

- Come.

The door opened little by little and Father Patrick

Doonican came slowly in.

- I was wondering if I could have a few words with you, Father?

- Yes. Yes. Come in, Patrick. Sit down. What is it?

Father Doonican edged onto the high-backed chair facing the older priest's desk. - It's about the complaint that Mister Doherty made to you, Father.

- Yes, what about it?

- Well, I called to see Mister McGrotty today, said Father Doonican, - and I told him I was starting to feel a bit apprehensive about the whole thing.

- Oh, he knows? What did he say?

- He said maybe I had cause to be. He thinks now with Arthur Corscadden being appointed to All Saints that Mister Doherty might have grounds for action against me. You know, for defamation.

- I can see that, said Father Babb. He sighed and rubbed his closed eyes with the backs of his fingers. A shiver passed through him. That's it, he thought. I've caught something.

- You were very foolish, Patrick, he said. - What in under heaven possessed you to say such a thing to Mister a....

- Mister Kelly. Brian Kelly.

- Brian Kelly. What in under heaven? And you a member of the interviewing panel.

Father Doonican cleared his throat and swallowed several times before answering.

- Well, Brian Kelly told me, you see, that Doherty wasn't applying for the job so I thought in the circumstances, you know, that there was no harm in saying it.

128

Something approaching confidence entered into his voice.
- And, to be honest, with Brian going overboard in his praise
of Doherty, I just couldn't resist stating the obvious.

- What's so obvious about it?

- Well, I knew you didn't think too much of him. I've
heard you say so.

- Yes, but a dangerous influence! Bent on destroying the
school! How in heaven's name did you come up with that?

- I didn't say *bent* on destroying the school. I said he *would*
destroy the school.

- Okay. *Would* destroy the school. How did you come up
with that?

- Well, said Father Doonican. - I'd no direct evidence as
such. But I had it on good authority.

- Whose?

- Mister McGrotty's. *He* told me.

Father Babb stood and pushed his chair to the side. He
walked back and forward across the length of the room for a
minute with his hands clasped tightly behind his back. Then
he stopped suddenly, turned quickly and said - Tell me. If you
were taken to court on this, would you implicate Ciaran
McGrotty?

- I don't know, answered Father Doonican. - I'm not sure.
But I'm hoping it won't come to that.

- Why so?

- I don't think, said Father Doonican, - that Brian Kelly is
in a proper state to sign an affidavit and then give evidence,
you know, after the death of his wife and all. The word is, he's
not getting over it.

Father Babb stood at the window and looked steadily across at the young priest.

- Well, in that case, he said, - you'll be all right, won't you?

- Yes, except....

- Except what?

- Except Ciaran was telling me that Brian was up in arms about not being shortlisted for a job in Star of the Sea....

- Yes?

- ...and he was going to go to the bishop to complain....

- Mm.

- ...but Ciaran thinks he's managed to put him off the idea.

Father Babb sighed. After a few moments he said - I think maybe we should just let the hare sit.

- Yes, Father.

- Unless....

- Yes, Father?

Father Babb gave a tight smile. - Unless you can think of something that might resolve the situation. Maybe if you....

He stared out the window. Bulging black clouds hung above the town, rising and spreading.

Dear God. That's the city centre.

A line of flames spurted silently from a smoke-covered shopping block.

That could be Waterloo Place. Or the Strand Road.

- Yes, Father?

Father Doonican was looking quizzically at him, mouth in a small circle.

- Ah, nothing. Let the hare sit.

- Yes. Yes, Father.

Father Doonican half rose, one knee stiffly bent.

- If that's all, Father, he said.

- Yes, that's all.

The young priest stood up and walked to the door. He opened it and then turned, remembering that he hadn't said thanks. But as he turned, the older priest was suddenly beside him, friendly and confidential.

- There is one other thing, said Father Babb. - I'm.... I'm not feeling the best today.

- Oh, I'm sorry to—

- I think.... I think I may be taking a dose of the flu.

- Oh dear. I'm sorry to hear that.

- I was due to say half seven mass this evening, continued the older priest, - and I was wondering if you'd fill in for me.

- Surely, Father. No problem. Was there anything in particular you want me to say in the homily?

- Ah no. Unless.... unless you have anything on Saint Joseph? Today's his feast day, as you know.

- Yes, I know. I was going to speak on him tomorrow anyway.

- That's great. You don't mind?

- Not at all. I'm delighted to help.

- Good, Patrick. That'll be all. And thanks.

- Not at all. Thank *you*.

- Just one last thing, said Father Babb. - You won't mention what happened in Andersonstown today, won't you not? You know, in your homily.

- Oh no.

- Fine. I'll be dealing with that tomorrow.

- I understand. Thank you, Father.

The door closed behind Father Doonican. Father Babb walked slowly to his chair and leaned forward against the back of it. His legs felt heavier now. He heard the dull crack of plastic bullets. Those foolish people. Pawns in the power bid. And they come out like lemmings every time.

He went to the window again. The day had faded and an early dusk had darkened the city. Much of what he could see was in flames, yet cars still moved steadily through treacherous streets. Patrick was earnest at heart. He was immature and impulsive sometimes but he would learn. He wanted to get on. That was good. The Church needed ambitious priests.

The homily was complete. He wouldn't change a word of it. Facts with fire, that's what the faithful want. They want to know. Shun the silver-tongued serpents, treasure the hard-won freedom of your religion and obey the laws of the land. Otherwise, the centre cannot hold.

He sat down and dialled one digit on the phone.

- Hello. Margaret, this is Father Babb. I'm not feeling very well. I think I may be taking the flu. Yes. Thanks, Margaret. No, I won't be down for dinner. Would you keep it in the oven for me? Good girl. Listen. I'm not to be disturbed. That's right. I'm going to lie down for a bit. Yes. Just one other thing. Would you bring me up half a glass of boiled water and some cloves? Yes, three or four will do. And a teaspoon of sugar. Thanks, Margaret.

He replaced the receiver and went to the window again. Without looking out he drew the curtains. Then he disconnected the phone.

The dream, when it happened, was stark. Nothing overlapped, nothing confused. *The mass has barely begun and the lookout comes running, his eyes filled with sleep and shame. The soldiers are coming, so close that we can see their horses' breath above the nearest brow. There are arguments and tears but the people are obedient. They take the sacred vessels and the altarcloth with them and I hurry down the brackened slope to meet the advancing troops. They lash me to the rock where moorland ferns and petals of scattered snowdrops lie crushed beneath my back. I scream the beginning of a prayer till the pain in my melting body closes my mind. I open my eyes and look for the face of God but all that I see is the darkness and the smallest slit of streetlight shifting on my bedroom wall.*

The silverhaired bug-eyed little man sat near the door caressing an empty glass.

- Is it you, Packie? said Myles, squinting over at him.

- It's me all right, excep I'm not too sure Pat knows I'm here. I'm sittin ten minutes here waitin for me B and P so I am.

Pat quickly sprang into a state of fuss and emerged from behind the bar carrying a brandy and port.

- You'll thank me for this someday, he said. - You're better spacin out them kinda drinks, you know.

- Christ of Almighty, snorted Packie. - Ye're startin to sound like me specialist. I came in here to forgit about him.

- How are you anyway, Packie? said Myles. - I heard you were in the hospital.

Packie put the glass to his mouth for a few seconds, then lowered it and smiled. - That's good stuff there so it is.

Myles went over and sat beside him.

- I didn't know you were out.

- Aye, I jist got out yistirday. I'm supposed to be off the drink but I took a fierce fit of the indigestion after me dinner this evenin and I thought maybe a wee Hennessy and port might settle me.

- Nothin better, said Myles. - It's good to see you anyway. I must say you're lookin well.

Packie puffed gently on a cigarette and then rested it on the ashtray. The smoke swirled around him like interweaving strands of fleece.

- Aye. Could be worse, he said.

Holding a damp cloth Pat moved along the front of the bartop rubbing circles on the shining surface. He blinked as he searched his memory.

- Is it Mister Howard the heart man? he asked. - Is that the one you're talkin about?

- Naw, said Packie. - Mister Fraser. Howard's dead. Sure he died three or four weeks ago there.

- You don't say. Cancer, was it?

- Cornery.

- It's supposed to be a very stressful job that, said Myles.

- D'ye know somethin? went on Packie. - I buried a doctor and two specialists this past year. Did ye know that?

- Right enough? said Myles.

134

- Aye. Doctor McAdams was the first wan. D'ye member him? Very strict sort of a boy. Always gittin on to ye. And Mister Howard and Mister Slocombe the liver man.

- I nivir heard of him now, said Pat, narrowing his eyes.

- Slocombe.

- Aw, *he* was a gentleman, said Packie. - A gentleman. I was at his funeral too, ye know.

- Were you now? said Myles.

- I was. Jist after Christmas there.

He shivered. - I nivir liked funerals.

- I can't say I'm too fond of them myself, agreed Myles. - Very morbid things.

- They are, said Packie. - They remind ye, ye see.

He held up his glass to check the level of liquor. - But them two were two good men. And I suppose McAdams meant well. I wouldn't want to be speakin ill of the dead.

He picked up the cigarette and the ash from it collapsed on his knees. - Do ye know this? The time of the last funeral, Mister Howard it was, I kep thinkin of the warnins they gave me. They all towl me the same thing. If I didn't start gittin a bit of exercise I wouldn't see the year out. That's what they all towl me. Aw, very depressin things, funerals.

- When was that? asked Pat, winking at Myles. - When did they say that to you, Packie?

- Aw Jesus, they were sayin that from ivir I remember. But, to tell ye the truth, the oney exercise I got this past twelve month was walkin back and forrard to the cemetery.

Pat laughed through his nose. - I'd say you're makin that one up, Packie.

135

- I am not. Sure I'm destroyed with the arthuritis. How do they expeck ye to git exercise if ye're destroyed with the arthuritis?

- I meant to go and see you on Thursday there, said Myles.

- Aye?

- Yeah. Myself and Conn Doherty were out seein Danny Leonard.

- Aw aye. I heard about Danny. How's he doin?

- He's very down, said Myles. - They're goin to save the leg all right but he's very down. I was sayin to you anyway. I meant to call up and see you but I got so annoyed lookin at Danny it went out of my head.

- Ah ye're all right, said Packie. He swallowed the remainder of his drink and held up the empty glass to show it to Pat. - D'ye see all this bother? The shootin and all? D'ye see when ye're in the ospital? When ye're in the ospital it's all different. Ye see things different.

- I'd say that's true, said Myles.

- Ye know what happened the time I was there? They brung in this reserve policeman half dead. He was riddled so he was. The IRA or INLA, I don't know which of them it was done it. And then wait till ye hear. The very nixt day they brung in that Sinn Féin man, what d'ye call him. Ye know yer man that got shot in revenge.

- Aye, said Pat, snapping his fingers. - I know who you're on about.

- I nivir seen them meself, went on Packie, - but somebody was tellin me they were right nixt door to wan another roarin outa them. And oney a wall between them.

136

- I know what you mean, said Pat.

He pointed at Packie. - I'll tell you now who that Sinn Féin man was.

- It just made me think, said Packie. - D'ye see if ye've got yer health, that's all that counts. Cigarette?

- Naw thanks. I don't smoke, said Myles.

- Nothin's worth it, said Packie. - D'ye want to know this? D'ye see if ye towl me now there'd be no more shootin or bombin, I'd settle for the British stayin here for the nixt hundred years.

- You're never goin to get anythin sorted out, said Myles, - as long as Thatcher's in power.

- Face like a bucket, said Pat.

- Ye're right there, agreed Packie. - All yer woman cares about is herself and that son of hers. Mark isn't it ye call him?

- God bless the mark, said Myles.

- Spoiled brat so he is. And she thinks there's nobody like him.

- Face like a bucket, said Pat.

- Ye're right there, said Packie

Mister McGrotty's voice was a monotone.

- It's been three months now, he said, - and I'm still waiting for your weekly notes.

Brian Kelly stood at the door of his classroom and stared disbelievingly.

- Notes! he whispered. - You're askin me for notes after

137

what happened.

The headmaster looked at Brian with expressionless eyes.

- Your wife died more than three months ago and I've been very patient. If you were well enough to put in an application for the Star of the Sea job then you're certainly well enough to do your notes.

- That was....

- Yes?

- That was... I was... Leave me alone. I've a class to teach here.

- You have to show me evidence of lesson preparation. I'm accountable to school inspectors, you know.

- I can't believe... I can't believe....

- And then you were able to sit sniggering with Conn Doherty at an Education Guidelines meeting last month. No, I think you're well capable of doing what all the rest of the staff have been doing without complaint.

- What's wrong with you? Brian whispered. - Is your mind sick or what?

He swung round to the class suddenly and shouted - Quiet there! Another sound and you're all gettin double homework!

He looked again at his headmaster. - What's the matter with you anyway? I've been teachin eighteen years and you're lookin for notes as if I was a student or somethin. Are you so insecure you can't tell inspectors that you trust your teachers?

Mister McGrotty moved as if to leave and then on the half-turn he stopped and said - Gerry McEldowney will be taking this class for language development in....

He looked at his watch.

\- in less than ten minutes. I'll want you in my office then.

\- What do you mean?

\- I want to issue you with a formal written warning and I'm not going to do it here.

\- What! What are you talking about?

\- I've nothing more to say for now, said Mister McGrotty. - Ten minutes then.

With that he turned away and strode purposefully down the corridor to his office.

Brian sat alone and opened his eyes. Once again the staffroom spun around him. He gripped the corner of the table and held it hard. The chair legs screeched along the floor as he stood up. Then he focused on the nearest window frame until each edge became a single line. He walked slowly back and forward for a minute and then left the staffroom. When he got to Billy Lambon's door he knocked and entered.

\- Hello Brian, said Billy.

\- Listen. You have to help me.

\- What's wrong? said Billy. – Here, take it easy. You look terrible.

\- McGrotty's houndin me over these notes I haven't done. He's out to get me. He says he's goin to give me a formal warnin right away.

\- My God. Are you serious?

\- Would you go to his office and tell him to leave me

alone? Please, Billy. I need time. You're my union rep. You have to do somethin. The man's a monster.

- I'll go and see him.

- Will you go now? Please. I shouldn't be in school at all. I need to get away. I can't handle this.

- I'll go right now. Don't worry.

- Thanks, Billy.

Brian went back to the staffroom and sat at the table. In his head he heard the hard rumble of his breath and staunched the tears that were rising. He closed his eyes to try and see her.

Julie, my angel, if I could touch you, kiss you, feel your breath on me just this once, just this one more time. Please, Julie, I know you're there. I'm lonely here. It's so lonely here. Do you remember the day you gathered flowers and put them in my hair and then you ran till I caught you? And at night miraculous you stood undressing while I lay waiting. But I learned love late, Julie, years late. And then when I'd learnt it I stood and watched them bury you in the dark wet of the clay. I left you behind and drove away. And the whispering children in the back were so forlorn and all I could think of was you. And still all I can think of is you. And the traffic lights on the Strand Road went green and amber and red again and again and again because everybody else's lives go on and there are things that never stop. Maybe I'll sleep tonight, Julie. Last night I nearly slept and then I thought about you and the cold stones and the black web in the clay and I wondered if I did very wrong for this to happen.

- Mister Kelly.

The headmaster was standing in front of him holding a

sheet of paper in the air.

- You were supposed to come to my office. Why did you not come?

Mister McGrotty's face was tight and pale. The paper waved and trembled in his hand. Brian half rose from the chair. He tried to speak but all that came was a gargle. He swallowed quickly, then coughed and said - Get away. Get away from me. Billy told you there now. You're not allowed. You can't do this.

- Billy? You mean Billy Lambon? Billy Lambon told me nothing of the sort.

- But he did. He went to your office and told you to leave me alone. You can't do this.

- Who are you to tell me what I can or cannot do! I met Billy in the corridor just now and he didn't speak about you. Now.

The headmaster came close to Brian and jabbed the air in front of his face. He hit the sheet of paper with the back of his free hand and snapped - I've taken as much as I'm going to take from you.

- *You've* taken! *You've* taken!

Brian stood up and gripped Mister McGrotty's shoulder with one hand.

- You! You!

His breath shuddered and his heart hammered in his head. - You come into this school and sit there in that office all day doin damn all. And you think you've some sort of divine right to look down your nose at the rest of us. You're a disgrace!

- How dare you! shouted Mister McGrotty. - Let me go!

- You wormed your way into that job. Everyone knows.

- Get back from me!

- You're earnin money under false pretences. You boasted at the last staff night that you pay more in tax than I take home. And what do you do? What do you do?

- Let me go!

- You're out at funerals five days a week buryin people you wouldn't even have talked to in the street. What are you anyway? You're not human!

- That's enough of that! shouted Mister McGrotty. He pointed a finger close to Brian's nose. - I'll take no more insubordination from you! Going round all day with that long face on you. You'd think you were the only one that ever had a death in the family. Well, let me tell you now—

- You'll tell me nothin, shouted Brian. - You wouldn't even let me grieve. You made me come back too soon. You made me....

- You're nothing but a whimpering excuse for a man, hissed the headmaster.

Brian felt one of his legs go numb and he put a hand on the table.

- Help! shouted Mister McGrotty.

Brian slumped down into the chair, his eyes and nose streaming.

The staffroom door opened and Father Patrick Doonican came in.

- I saw that, he said briskly.

Mister McGrotty stood limply against a wall rubbing his shoulder.

- You saw what? shouted Brian.

- I saw, repeated the priest. He went over to the headmaster and said - Are you all right?

- What's happenin? whispered Brian. - What's happenin here?

- I saw, said Father Doonican. - I'm reporting you.

- You're nothin but a piece of shit, shouted Brian, trying to rise. - Get out of my sight! Get out of my sight the two of you!

Myles Corrigan was holding court.

- Work, he announced, - is the biggest con trick those bastards in Westminster ever played on us.

- It's all right for you to talk, said Michael. - You don't have to work. You got compensation and a big lump sum.

- Aye, and don't you git a teacher's pension every month too? said Pat. - From the British government?

Myles nodded. - That's right. And sick money and disability livin allowance as well. Sure I bought a field in Donegal.

- That's the place you call your welfare estate, isn't it? said Pat.

- For God's sake, said Michael. - You don't have to work at all. You're landed so you are.

- It still doesn't change what I'm sayin, Myles said patiently. - Nobody should have to work. The whole scheme was started by the Methodists.

- The Methodists? I nivir knew that now, said Packie, pulling a twenty packet from the cigarette machine.

- Yeah, continued Myles. - John Wesley and the boys. They told the people if they didn't work hard they'd all end up in hell. So the government latched onto it and turned the whole country into slaves. Low wages, long hours, too exhausted to ask questions. And then they'd this place colonised, you see. And their planters got the system goin here.

- Is that why the Prods are so hardworkin then? asked Packie.

- It is, said Myles. - Hardworkin. Efficient. Upstandin. No time to think. And that's why most of the best Irish writers are Catholics. Never did a day's work in their lives. Late-risin depraved lazy bastards.

Michael laughed. - James Joyce wasn't like that, was he? he asked.

Myles gave a little snort. - James Joyce? For fuck sake. Joyce was the worst jobseeker this country ever saw. And the biggest scrounger. You know all the stuff about him leavin Ireland so he could write properly? A load of brock. Most of Dublin was after him for money he owed them. That's why he never came back. That's why he kept shiftin round Europe like a blue-arsed fly. Always one country ahead of the Dublin and district debt recovery boys.

- You're havin us on, said Michael.

- What are you talkin about? said Myles. He tapped his glass on the bar and gave Pat a nod. - Joyce worked in a bank in Rome for two weeks and he was never the same after it. Half his internal organs collapsed. What the fuck are you laughin at? It was months before he could lift a pen again.

- Jesus, said Pat and slid the drink towards Myles. - And you're tellin us it was the Methodists started that.

- Work, you see, said Myles. - It was like a foreign body that got into his system. It damn well nearly killed him.

- There's a man now'll tell us if that's true or not, said Packie.

Conn Doherty closed the door behind him and took off his overcoat.

- What are you on about, Packie? he asked.

- Myles is sayin here that James Joyce the writer nivir worked a day in his life excep for workin in a bank for.... how long was it, Myles?

- Two weeks and two days, said Myles.

- I don't know, said Conn. - I thought he taught in Dublin for a while. And then in Paris he taught English as a foreign language. As far as I know anyway.

Marcus McHale twitched with irritation. - You wudn't turn up the sound on that TV, wud you, Pat?

The volume rose and Myles said to Conn - How's tricks?

- Not great, answered Conn. He raised his voice. - Pat, would you put on a Guinness for me?

- Up and comin.

Conn went to their corner and sat down. Myles followed him, Jameson in hand.

- What d'you mean, not great?

- Brian Kelly was suspended today, said Conn.

- He what!

- McGrotty provoked him into doin somethin,

145

supposedly assaultin him. Father Doonican says he saw it happenin.

- Jesus.

- Brian told me McGrotty got him into a terrible state over notes and all he remembers is cryin about Julie. He doesn't remember touchin McGrotty or anythin.

- That McGrotty's an evil bastard, breathed Myles. - Imagine doin that.

- Father Babb and Josie Rabbitt were on the job right away and they suspended Brian till further notice.

- Have they the power to do that?

- I don't know, said Conn. - They must have. They're chairman and vice-chairman.

- Do they not need a quorum? Surely they need more than two members of the board to do a drastic thing like that?

- I don't know, said Conn. - They probably do. You're probably right.

- What about his union?

Conn shook his head. - Brian told me he tried to get Billy Lambon to keep McGrotty away from him. He's the union rep.

- And what?

- Lambon never went near McGrotty. I asked him about it and he said Brian never asked him to do anythin.

- Why would he lie? asked Myles. - Or is he lyin?

- Oh he's lyin all right. Brian's honest to a fault.

- Why's he lyin then? persisted Myles.

- I don't know. Maybe he was scared to go to McGrotty. Most of the staff are scared of him.

146

Myles looked at his untouched whiskey. He picked it up and left it down again. - Is there not another job goin in All Saints? Is there not a vacancy for vice-principal?

Conn slapped the table. - Jesus, that's it!

- Comin now, Conn, shouted Pat.

Michael came part of the way across the floor and pointed at the television set.

- Did yous hear that? he said.

- What? asked Myles.

- On the news there. They're arrestin people rings round them for killin the two corporals. They've impounded all the newsreel that was taken and they're liftin everybody that was anywhere near the car.

- Surprise surprise, said Myles.

- There were people there thought it was goin to be Milltown cemetery all over again, said Michael. He shook his head disgustedly and went back to the bar. Myles called after him - Are you not sittin down with us, Michael?

- I'll be over in a minute. Hold on.

Myles stared at the pictures on the TV.

- How about that? he said.

- We should have known it was goin to happen, said Conn.

Myles gave a quick sniff. - Yeah. Looks like the curtains are comin down early on *Gibraltar* and *Milltown*.

- And *The Corporals*'ll soon be playin to packed courthouses.

- I don't know about you, Conn, but I reckon this one could run longer than *The Mousetrap*.

- I've a bad feelin about this, said Conn.

- Be patient, said Gus Hazlitt. - They'll be here.

Conn looked at his watch. - I don't think so. It's a quarter to four.

- Maybe it's inconvenient for people, said Annette Givens. - I know it's inconvenient for me.

- They all agreed, insisted Conn. - I picked today because it was the day that suited everybody.

- Could they have forgotten, do you think? said Angela McDonald.

Conn just about stifled a sneer. - I sent round a note this mornin to remind everybody. Sure you got it yourself.

- Well, said Gus, prolonging the word for no obvious reason.

Conn drew a deep breath. - Can we start the meetin? Okay? I'll get straight to the point. Brian Kelly was suspended indefinitely a week ago for an alleged assault on Mister McGrotty. This suspension was out of order because it was decided on without a quorum. However, within two days a full meetin of the board of governors ratified the suspension.

Billy Lambon coughed. - Excuse me. If you don't mind my sayin, surely at this point it's irrelevant whether or not the original suspension was out of order? Brian's now suspended and properly so.

- The point I'm makin, said Conn, - is that Father Babb and Mister Rabbitt were a bit overenthusiastic with their

148

original decision. I think that may point to somethin interestin. And I have to say, Billy, I don't accept the word properly is exactly appropriate. This whole thing may well have been cooked up.

Gus frowned disapprovingly. - I think we all have to be very careful about how we say things here. We don't know exactly what happened. Therefore we shouldn't judge.

- Brian's been judged, snapped Conn. - Do we stand aside and do nothin?

- He assaulted Mister McGrotty, said Angela. - He, how would you say....

Conn couldn't wait. - How do we know McGrotty's not lyin? How do we know Doonican's not lyin? Does it not even seem possible to you that the two people who could be nailed for defamin my character just happened to be involved in somethin that could end up silencin the unfortunate witness to that defamation?

- We have to deal in the truth, said Gus, shaking his head sadly. - And I wouldn't be so hasty if I were you, Conn, about accusin other people of lyin. You're not without stain, you know.

Conn glared at Gus. - What? I misinterpreted? I embellished? How do you know I wasn't right?

Gus breathed in and out hard two or three times until something like serenity settled on him. - I didn't think I'd need to say this in front of others, but you spread it around some of the staff this week that you saw Mister McGrotty and Father Babb havin a good laugh together just after Brian was suspended. And then you admitted to me that they may well just have been sharin a joke about somethin unconnected.

- Or maybe the two of them had indigestion, said Conn, - and they just *looked* as if they were gloatin.

- Can I say somethin here? said Billy. - I'd like to say somethin here. I don't think— how many people have we at this meetin?— I don't think five people can pass a motion on anythin. I mean, there's twenty-two on the staff apart from Mister McGrotty and Brian and five of us can hardly be considered representative.

- The other seventeen have abstained, retorted Conn. - For their own reasons they've abstained. That's what their absence means. We can pass anythin we want.

- Okay, said Billy. - But at the end of the day we can't really achieve anythin. The union aren't interested in pursuin this. They questioned Brian and he admitted he doesn't remember what he did to Mister McGrotty. And two reputable witnesses say he was guilty of assault.

- Reputable! breathed Conn. He stared at Billy, eyes bulging. - Reputable! he repeated. - Don't make me laugh! And don't try to tell me the Irish Catholic Teacher's Association is neutral. We all know where *they* stand.

The room went still. After a few seconds Billy said quietly - I'm not going to dignify either of those remarks with a reply.

Angela shook her head reprovingly at Conn. - Just because you're in a British union that's far removed from the hard graft that Billy's involved in doesn't give you the right to... to....

- I don't like this name-callin, said Annette. - I think we should try and get away from this name-callin.

Her tone suddenly changed from the plaintive to the

assertive. - But there was somethin far more important I wanted to say.

- Could I go now? said Angela, beginning to rise. - My two children are waitin for me in the car park.

- We all know, continued Annette, - that Brian has been actin strangely since his wife died. What'shername.

- Julie, said Conn.

- Julie. And I don't know what he told anybody else but he told me there's somethin the matter with his health and it hasn't been diagnosed yet. A.... ammm....

- Yes? prompted Gus.

- What I mean is, he's under stress and it's a terrible pity about him. But...I don't like to say it... but... people are sayin he's becomin unstable.

- Aye, said Conn. - I've heard that word mentioned two or three times this past week myself. I wonder who started it?

- What do you mean? said Billy sharply.

- Well, it's the kind of smear I would expect from certain people on the board—

- Hold on there, interrupted Gus.

- and you all know what label the Soviets put on the problem people before they send them to Siberia.

- What? said Angela, standing, handbag in hand.

- Unstable. Unbalanced. That's what they call them.

Gus closed a large notebook that lay on the table in front of him and clipped his biro into his breast pocket.

- There's a hidden agenda here, he said.

- What are you talkin about? snapped Conn.

- There's a hidden agenda here. Conn, you have a lot of

good qualities but— I'm goin to be frank— you've got a serious hang-up about authority. I used to think it was just a healthy cynicism but I think now that I was wrong.

- It depends what sort of authority you're talkin about, said Conn.

- I'm talkin about authority. It doesn't matter whether it's spiritual or temporal. You just seem to like attackin it. And, quite honestly, I don't see why the rest of us should be associated with this kind of disrespect.

- That's it, said Annette. - I'm goin.

- I'm goin too, said Billy. - This isn't gettin us anywhere.

- Yes? the woman said, rubbing her hands on her apron.

- I was lookin for one of the priests, said Brian. - Do you think....

- Let me see. Father Taggart's upstairs watching the rugby but I think Father O'Dea came in there just a few minutes ago. I'll go and see if I can find him. Oh dear, what's the matter?

Brian was standing suddenly stiff, his face white with fear.

- It's the cat, he said hoarsely. - I'm allergic to them.

A large sleek-black cat had stopped to rub its side along Brian's shin, its whiskers twitching contentedly.

- Oh, said the woman. She leaned down and waved at the animal. - Go, Cuddles, she ordered. -Away now.

Cuddles looked up at her with lazy disdain, blinked twice and moved royally on.

- He's the family pet, she explained. - We're all very fond of him. He's a lovely tom.

Brian muffled a sneeze in the palm of his hand. - Sorry, he said. - It's this allergy.

- Oh I know, I know. I had a brother a greengrocer in Belfast, and he—

- Sorry. Could I wait outside? asked Brian. - I don't know where he's gone. I think he might still be around. I'm sorry. I'm a bad case.

- Not at all. Not at all. Frank — he's dead now, God rest him — he couldn't abide them. He used to say... All right. You wait outside and I'll tell Father O'Dea you're here.

Brian hurried through the high front doorway of the Carmelite retreat centre and around the side of the building. His eyes pricked and streamed and his arms itched to the bone. He stopped at a summer seat and sat down, dabbing his face with a handkerchief. A little gust of wind lifted some hairs on the back of his neck and a bird in a bush bounced on what seemed like a leaf. He stared rigidly ahead and the Foyle curled quietly along the valley. A sudden wave of sunlight turned the river to silver and took the sight from his eyes. He closed them and felt a hard irritation there as if they'd just been peppered with grit. His breath shortened and he opened his eyes slowly, painfully. Cuddles was straddling his right shoe lengthways, scratching its belly, maybe even masturbating, on the leather and the laces. Brian jerked his foot violently and a jagged black shadow flew screaming into the brightness, lingered there for a moment and then came down. Close to the end of the descent its head crashed against

153

the open edge of a wheelbarrow handle and it landed on its side in the clay. And there it lay, still.

Could be a fractured skull, thought Brian. That would be good. Or maybe he's dead. That would be good too.

Father O'Dea stepped from the white light and looked in disbelief at the fallen cat.

- My God, he said weakly. - What have you done?

He stooped to examine Cuddles and then turned to Brian.

- What have you done? he said again and suddenly Cuddles was up and away, one life to the bad, complaining as he went.

Father Taggart seemed to have all day.

- If that's the case, he said, - then why don't you take the advice of...what was his name?

- Conn Doherty.

- Why don't you take the advice of Conn Doherty? Giving evidence in support of his action would bring justice to him and it would give you....

The priest closed his eyes for a moment.

- ...What's the word? It would give you the satisfaction of exposing these people.

- I know, said Brian. - I know it would.

- Catharsis, said the priest and he smiled brightly, revealing two rows of perfect tiny teeth. - That's the word I'm looking for. You'd be rid of all this anger and aggro that's eating you up.

Brian looked at him with a weary frustration. - The only thing is, Father, I've got a terrible fear of them, you see. I just have the certain feelin that sometime, when all this is in the past, they'd get back at me. When nobody's lookin, when everybody's forgotten.

Father Taggart leaned forward enthusiastically. - Surely, Brian, they'd think twice about victimising you again after you'd shown them what you're capable of.

- Maybe. Maybe you're right, Father. If it was only three or four people you'd be right. But it's...it's...it's an institution. Sorry. I shouldn't be sayin that.

The priest smiled again, a warm open smile. - Not at all. Not at all. Just because I belong to a club doesn't mean I'm always happy with the way it's run.

His eyes twinkled and his shoulders shook in self-approval.

- These people don't amount to much by themselves, said Brian. - But they're protected. It's as if no matter what they do they're goin to be protected. I've only been thinkin lately there must have been other ones that suffered before me.

- You're right, said the priest, nodding. - I'm sure you're right there.

This is such a good man, Brian thought. Why can't they all be like that?

- And there's somethin that really annoys me, Father, he said, - and I haven't the words to come back at them. I've friends— I'm not talkin about Conn Doherty, although he's a friend too— and they're tellin me I'm lucky not to have been sacked after what happened. They're sayin I should let the

155

whole thing go. And these are my best friends. It's like it's a conspiracy and they don't even know they're part of it.

- You're going to fight it, aren't you?

- I can't. How can I?

- Of course you can.

- No, Father.

Brian's lips were tight and thin.

- No, Father, he repeated. - I'm goin to let it happen. I'm goin to offer it up to God for ... I don't know ... as atonement for all the things I've done wrong.

Father Taggart frowned and gave a long slow sigh.

- You can't offer hatred up to God, Brian, he said. - Because that's what you'd be doing, you know. You told me you hated them, the guilty ones. You can't offer that up.

Brian sat slumped, his head deep in his shoulders. Neither of them spoke for some time. The only sounds in the room came from outside, the birdsong, the toot of a horn, the thud of a boot on a ball.

Father Taggart spoke again.

- If you're not going to give evidence in court, then there's only one other thing you can do.

- What's that, Father?

- Forgive. Yes. It's not impossible. It's something we all have to learn, over and over again, each new time.

Brian closed his eyes. There were different tears there now, away at the back, in with the grit.

- Forgiveness is a very practical thing, said the priest. - It really is. These people that are hammering you are unfeeling and unscrupulous. They don't care how much you hate them.

156

There's only one person it harms.

- Me.

- Yes. Well, I suppose not just you. Your children are bound to be affected too, aren't they?

Brian stared ahead, out the window behind the priest, at the dark oak trees and the wide sky beyond. He shuddered.

- Aye, he said. - And then there's God. Isn't there?

- No one knows when his time's going to come, Brian. No one should take the risk of meeting his Maker with hatred in his heart.

Suddenly and preposterously, the priest laughed. It was spontaneous and unguarded and Brian almost felt like laughing too without knowing why.

- What is it, Father? he asked, smiling respectfully.

- I was thinking that I probably sound like one of those hellfire priests that used to come to give retreats in Derry.

- You did, a bit.

- But I'm forgetting. This started off as Confession. And it just occured to me that you're going to have to tell me a real sin. I know we both used the word hatred but I think now we were wrong. I've only known you for less than an hour, Brian, but I'm certain now that you're simply not capable of hatred. Anger, yes. Outrage, definitely. And both of those are justified.

- So what do I do?

- Well, I can't give you absolution unless you can dig out a proper sin from somewhere.

Brian wrinkled his forehead.

Father Taggart laughed again. - Surely a man of your

experience shouldn't have much difficulty coming up with one.

There was silence for a minute and then Brian brought his lips together to suppress a smile.

- I've got one, he said.

- Good, said the priest.

- But it's twenty years old. Is that all right?

- Fire away.

- In April of sixty-eight, when I got my scholarship cheque for the summer term in the teachers' trainin college, I blew every last bit of it on a horse called Redemption.

The priest laughed happily.

- You're making that up, he said.

- As God's my witness, said Brian, - a three-year-old filly called Redemption.

- I just think it's ridiculous, that's all, said Myles.

Conn frowned and shook his head. - I'm not arguin.

- Everybody off the hook. Just because he's afraid of goin to hell he calls them all in one by one and forgives the whole fucken lot of them.

- He did what he thought was right, said Conn. - Give it a rest will you.

Myles nodded. - Okay. Sorry. I know you were close to him and all but surely you can see.

- I do see but I don't want to talk about it. For God's sake.

- All I can say is, went on Myles, - he's goin to get the quare shock when he doesn't waken up. Boy, will he be kickin himself.

- Is that drink nearly ready, Pat? shouted Conn.

- Up and comin.

- Imagine if the devil really existed, said Myles. - You know what I'd do? I'd make a pact with him that he'd let me torment that crowd for the rest of their lives.

Conn smiled bitterly.

- In return for what? he asked.

- In return for him existin. And then when the last bell sounded, then you'd see some justice done.

- It's trumpet.

- What do you mean?

- It's not the last bell. It's the last trumpet.

Myles raised his hand in acknowledgement. - Right. When Satchmo blew his trumpet I'd be singin *What a wonderful World* down at them.

Conn got up and went to the bar. Pat was proudly surveying the creamy head on the pint of Guinness that sat in front of him.

- What do you think? he asked.

- Perfect finish, said Conn. He felt an inane obligation to stand awhile admiring it. - It's a shame I have to drink it.

Pat leaned forward suddenly and held Conn's arm in a confidential vice. - I was very sorry to hear about that man outa your school, he said.

- Aye, it's rough.

- What was it? Cancer, was it?

- I don't know. I never asked.

- I saw the thing in the Derry Journal about him. That was a very nice thing. Was it you wrote it?

Conn shook his head. - It wasn't me.

- I wonder who it was did it? Was it the Journal do you think?

- Gus Hazlitt wrote it.

- You're jokin. Gus Hazlitt that used to drink here?

- Aye.

- That's a goodun. Gus Hazlitt. Anyway, it was very nice what he wrote.

- It was.

Pat loosened his grip slightly and lowered his voice to a throaty whisper, moving his head odorously closer.

- Did Myles tell you what happened here last night?

- How do you mean? asked Conn.

- Ast him about....

Pat took a deep breath and his shoulders began to shake with silent laughter.

- Ast him about the one from Omagh that tried it on with him here last night.

- Right enough?

- Aye. Just ast him about it.

Pat released Conn and snorted good-humouredly. - He's a real heartbreaker so he is. You'd nivir have known it.

When Conn arrived back at the table Myles had his head in The Guardian.

- I'm lookin at somethin here, he said. - Tell me what you think of this.

- Go ahead.

160

- It's a thing called E V P.

- What's that? said Conn.

- Electronic voice phenomenon. Accordin to this, you can use it to speak to the dead. All you need is a radio and a computer and a tape recorder.

- That sounds like one of those fillers they put into newspapers.

- I know it does, said Myles. - But wait till you hear. "Edison and Marconi both had a deeply religious belief that the dead could be contacted."

- There's two born again every minute.

- "Queen Victoria, Stan Laurel and President Kennedy have all been contacted."

- Are you sure that's not the National Enquirer you're lookin at?

- I know. I know. But listen. "To talk to a spirit, simply record some radio static for two or three minutes while callin down any dead person you want. Put the recordin into a computer, slow it down, then reverse it and listen with all your heart and soul. Because, and this is crucial, you must be a believer in the afterlife for this to work."

- That counts you out.

- I suppose it does. I suppose you're right, Myles said with a sigh. He folded the paper and threw it on the windowsill.

Conn coughed, carefully restrained a smile and said - Tell us. What's all this about you and some woman here last night?

Myles glowered over at the bar. - That bastard Pat. Where is he, the bastard? It was him told you, wasn't it?

161

- It was.

Myles picked up a beer mat and tore it into four strips.

- Naw, she was a real hoor, he said. - Nobody in their right mind would have gone off with her.

- Who was she anyway?

- This one that comes in some nights with the two great whites. You know the maneaters that land in here nearly every Thursday night.

- Aye. The two Doherty girls.

- Well, this one's Doherty as well. I think she's from up by Omagh. I don't know if you ever saw her.

- Long brown hair?

- That's the one. Wolfwoman.

- I've seen her, said Conn. - She's really sexy. A bit on the rough side but she's dead sexy.

- Yeah. She's rough all right. And ready.

- What happened anyway?

Myles looked up at the bar again. There was no sign of Pat. - I was sittin here doin nobody any harm and your woman comes over and sits down beside me without askin.

- A bit of a liberty, said Conn.

- She says, and I quote: "I've been watchin you all night, sailor, and I like what I see."

- Did you not tell her you weren't a sailor?

- I forgot. Anyway, I says to her, "Is that a fact now?" and she says right back, "I'd like to take you home with me and rattle you, sailor boy."

- Rattle you?

- Rattle me.

162

- Go ahead.

- "And don't worry", she says. "You won't be needin your galoshes." "Galoshes?" says I. "Rubbers", she says. "I'm on the pill."

- I hate these ones that never get past the small talk.

- "Any way you want it," she says.

- Good God.

- "I'll have you up all night," she says.

- Jesus, Myles. I know you're not makin this up. It's too ridiculous to make up.

- It knocked me back, I can tell you.

Conn reached over and took a beer mat from Myles' hands. - That's mine, he said. - I need that.

- Sorry.

- How'd it go with her anyway?

Myles stared at him. - What do you mean how did it go? It *didn't* go. *I* didn't go. D'you think for one minute I'd go bareback on that one? She'd have killed me.

- How'd she take it?

- Not too well. She called me a pig and went for my balls with her handbag—

- She attacked you?.

- but I'd them well hidden.

- Close encounter of the turd kind.

- And then she threatened to have me arrested for molestin her. Lucky there were witnesses.

- You should have said to her, "You can huff and puff all you want but by the hair on my chinny chin chin—"

- I know. I know. I thought of that about twelve hours

163

later. But she was away then.

Myles looked at the bar again and shouted - Hey Pat. I want you in here.

- In and comin, came the distant response.

Myles got up and went to another table. He came back with a collection of beer mats.

- What's happenin with you anyway? he said to Conn. - Should you not be somewhere else seein this is a Friday and all?

- Melanie, you mean?

- Yeah.

- She's away at a school reunion. But she's comin back to the house later.

- I meant to ask you this before. What age is she?

- Twenty-six.

- Do you not think she's a wee bit young for you?

- You know the way it is, said Conn. - Beggars can't be choosers.

He felt a hand on his shoulder and jumped a little in his chair. Pat was standing behind him humming tunelessly.

- Jesus. Where'd you come from? You seemed to come out of nowhere.

Pat left a glass of whiskey on the table. - A wee double on the house, Myles. Just for old times' sake.

- Fuck off, said Myles and picked up the drink. He smelt it and said - Fuck off now.

Pat smiled tolerantly. - I'm gittin a Guinness ready for you over there, Conn. Compliments of The Drunken Dog.

- Thanks, said Conn. - Take your time. I'm in no hurry.

Pat went away humming to himself.

- It's a funny thing about women, said Conn.

- What is?

- You wait for ages and then two of them come along one after the other.

- Two? said Myles and folded a beer mat in two. - You're not tellin me there's another?

- A sort of a way.

- What sort of a way?

Conn took a long drink from his glass to cover the smile that was coming.

- It's this girl Lucia McCaul I used to know, he said, wiping his mouth slowly with the palm of his hand. - Well, she's not a girl anymore. She's my age. Married and all. Grown-up family.

- Separated?

- Naw.

- That's dangerous territory, Conn.

- She rang me durin the week from Downpatrick. She's comin to Derry for a teachers' union conference and she wants to meet me.

- After how long?

- Thirty years. Just over thirty years.

- Jesus.

- Aye. I went with her in my first year trainin.

- And she wants to see you again.

- She does. She's very unhappy, she says, and somebody she met told her I was unattached. So she rang me up.

- Are you goin to meet her?

- I'm not sure. There's baggage there.

- Baggage?

- Aye. She was the first girl I ever went with and I never really got her out of my system.

- That first fine careless rapture.

- It wasn't so careless. I was a prude and she was normal and—

- Never the twain shall meet.

- She went with me for a few months and then she dumped me. I actually had a breakdown over it.

- Is that how it happened?

- Well, she wasn't the cause exactly, said Conn. He felt a brittleness starting in his voice and he raised the glass to his lips again.

- Mama Church controllin you, said Myles with a sniff.

- Aye. A combination of blood and thunder sermons and a biddable wee boy that took the rules too seriously. Lucia was only the final straw.

- So you don't blame her?

- Not really. It was circumstances. Just after she dumped me she went off with this real smoothie from Downpatrick that stayed in digs with me. She started sleepin with him nearly right away. It wasn't somethin that was done then. Not much anyway.

- Don't I know. So that did it.

- That finished me. Next stop Gransha hospital.

- I can understand, said Myles, - why you'd be curious to meet her. But—

- She married the smoothie, you know. And then she

166

discovered he was a real bastard. Womaniser. Chauvinist. All that. I could have told her. I could have told her he was in love with himself. I was stupid but I knew enough to know that.

The door swung open and a large group of girls moved brightly across the room. As they walked past they turned almost in unison to glance at the two men and then stood along the front of the bar whooping and laughing.

- Ah, said Myles. - If only she'd had the sense to see. But sure love's blind. Isn't it?

- That's the word she used on the phone. Blind. She cried, you know. She begged me to meet her. Actually begged.

- What did you say?

- I put her off. I told her to ring back next week.

- Well now girls, said Pat. - What'll it be?

- When's this conference she's comin to? asked Myles.

- It starts this day week and goes on all weekend.

- That's when you see Melanie, isn't it? The weekends?

- Aye.

- Right, said Pat. - Five bacardi and coke and two vodka and white. Sit yourselves down there girls. I'll be with yous in a minute.

- It's amazin about women, said Conn. - She still has my photo. Her and her husband spent nine years teachin in Zambia and she'd my photo with her. She took it half way round—

- Sorry for keepin you, Conn, said Pat and placed a Guinness in front of him.

He raised his voice. - Patience, girls. I'll be with yous in a tick.

- Thanks, Pat, said Conn.

Pat smiled. - That one's on the house, remember.

- Appreciated, Pat.

- Right, girls. Now just gimme the order again, if yous would.

- But I'll tell you what it's like, said Conn. - You know the way you look up at a star and it's not actually there anymore?

- Yeah.

- Well, that's the way she sees me. She looks at the photo and the boy she sees isn't there anymore.

- I get what you mean, said Myles. His eyes fell on the colours of the company opposite and lingered on the bare shoulders and dark dreamy eyes of the girl nearest him.

- So you've a big decision to make, he said to Conn.

- I don't know if it's that big. There's no hurry anyway. I've got till Wednesday. She's ringin on Wednesday.

- **Sorry. Do you mind?**

- **What?**

- **I just wanted to make a point, if that's all right.**

- **Who are you?**

- **Myles. It's Myles here.**

- **Myles who?**

- **Myles Corrigan, your main character.**

- **You're not making yourself clear.**

- **Sorry. It's just that I'm not at all happy about the way things are panning out.**

- What? What do you mean?

- Look. I gave in to being a heavy drinker. I went along with shitting myself, distasteful as it was. I didn't even mind being a bit of a buffoon sometimes.

- Buffoon. Yes.

- Everything was worth it because of my interesting past.

- Past? What past?

- You know. Eva and all. And my knowledge and my wit and my principles.

- Ah.

- And the way I can communicate with Conn. That's so refreshing. Two Irishmen communicating with each other.

- Yes?

- But now suddenly I'm so pathetic I can't even take up a once in a lifetime offer from a generous fun-loving girl. What I want to know is this. Am I gay? Is that it? Or am I impotent? Tell me. Or am I just not interested anymore? What is it that I'm supposed to be?

- Hold on. Are you from The Drunken Dog by any chance?

- My God. I'm Myles Corrigan. Your anti-hero. The greatest Irish character since Leopold Bloom. The raison d'être for your book.

- What book?

- This is ridiculous. Have you lost your memory or what?

- Oh yes. The book. I remember now. It's these drugs. Things flit in and out. They're treating me for schizophrenia. Did you know that?

- I don't believe it.

- It's true. I mean, it's true that they're treating me. It doesn't necessarily mean I have it. Does it?

- I'll tell you now if you have it or not.

- Yes. Yes. Tell me.

- Do you hear voices?

- Voices? Absolutely not.

- You don't have it then. It's what's called a misdiagnosis. I've heard of that happening before.

- Thank God. Or should I say thank you? You don't know how good it is to have someone to talk to.

- You don't have to worry anymore. I'm here now.

- This means so much to me. What did you say your name was?

- Dear God. What have they done to you?

- I'll tell you what they've done to me. Do you realise where we are?

- Where?

- This, my friend, is the secure unit of Gransha psychiatric hospital.

- Jesus. What are we doing here? You're not dangerous, are you?

- I don't think so. Although I was lifted by the police on the Strand Road one night.

- What for? What were you doing?

- All I was doing was asking people for directions to The Drunken Dog.

- Right?

- There was this big long giggle of girls all linked up in

a mazychain across the road and they told me I must be looking for The Silver Dog in Bishop Street.

- I see.

- And they kept pointing at me and hooting out of them.

- Why would that have been?

- Then this crowd of fellows left off beating the hell out of each other for a minute just to tell me The Drunken Duck was twenty miles over the border in Donegal.

- You'd lost your way. That's hardly grounds for locking you up.

- I know. But it seems all I had on at the time was a small lemon jockstrap.

- Oh I see. Well at least you weren't exposing yourself.

- I don't know about that. I had it on back to front.

- Inside out, you mean?

- Back to front.

- Christ.

- Stress. That's what it was. Stress and loss of memory—

- Of course. That can happen.

- brought on by....

- Yeah?

- ...brought on by...Hold on. It's coming.

- That's okay. Take your time. There's no hurry.

- Thanks. What were we talking about?

- You were going to tell me what it was that brought on your amnesia.

- I don't remember saying that.

- Easy now. Just stop and think.

- Got it! Writer's block. That was the whole bother. It's coming back to me now.

- What a terrible thing.

- I know. I sat for weeks looking at that blank page and I couldn't get any forrader.

- Forrader?

- Forrader. I was bogged down. Mired. Mudholed. Marooned. Trapped at the top of the page. Lost for words. All I had left was Conn's encounter with Lucia and Myles' suicide.

- Myles' what!

- Suicide. Either that or I was going to have him shot. A bit of predictable pathos on the one hand and Conn resolving all his spiritual hang-ups on the other. You know the kind of thing.

- O dear God.

- Exactly. It was too Hollywood, too everything coming together. You must remember, Conn. This book started out as a work of art. Now as you know, great literature has loose ends everywhere. Like life itself. But this hoor of a thing was threatening to turn into a glittery little music box tied up with pretty pink ribbons.

- I'm Myles. And listen. You have to change direction. Right away. For a start you need counselling.

- Out of the question.

- What do you mean?

- They simply don't have the manpower. The head psychiatrist's in a padded cell. Overwork. They got him out on the roof chasing cats. All they can do here is keep

172

shovelling drugs into us and wait for the next financial year. Did you not hear about the cutbacks for eighty-eight eighty-nine?

- I don't think so. I tend to switch off when that sort of thing comes on.

- They had to get rid of the goldfish. They can't even afford to run a fucking goldfish tank. Now that's serious.

- What about your literary agent? Could he not come and visit you?

- Don't talk to me. All that bastard wants is for me to be on talk shows. All he can think about is success. You think you know a person.

- Take it easy. Don't panic whatever you do.

- And my wife. Did I tell you about my wife?

- Walked out on you did she?

- Overdose of tranquillisers. She's in the physical hospital getting pumped. She's the only one would listen to me.

- Don't worry about it. Just try and keep this in perspective. James Joyce had a breakdown during Ulysses. Did you realise that? And he took sixteen years to write Finnegans Wake. Take your time. There's no rush. Art will out.

- I can't wait, Conn. These drugs have me destroyed.

- Myles. The name's Myles.

- I'm going to give it another week and if I can't think of an inconclusive ending by then I'm going to burn the manuscript.

- What! But you can't do that.

- Who says I can't?

- You've got a responsibility. You can't just wipe out your characters as if they never existed.

- I can do whatever I want. I'm a novelist. That's it. One week.

- Mister Joyce?

- Speaking. I'll be down now. Who's calling?

- It works!

- What works?

- Electronic voice phenomenon. It actually works!

- Say again.

- EVP. It's like a telephonic time machine.

- Very interesting.

- It's revolutionary, you know.

- Really? Does it carry the death penalty?

- Oh no, not at all. This is science.

- Ah.

- I'm so excited, Mister Joyce. Do you know that I've been trying to get through to you for the past five days?

- Hah! I tried to get through to people for a lot longer than that. It would make you weep.

- I understand what you mean. I've been doing my best to pass on your message for a long time myself. But here, I'd better introduce myself. My name is Myles Corrigan.

- Nice to talk to you, Myles.

- Thanks. Do you mind if I call you Jimmy?

- Yis I do mind as a matter of fact.

- Sorry. James, then. Is James all right?

- No it is not all right. My name is William. Heil Hitler!

- What!

- Heil Hitler!

- Hitler's dead.

- I know. Long live Hitler!

- My God.

- Tell me something, yis? Where and when are you speaking from?

- The north of Ireland. Nineteen eighty-eight.

- You mean Northern Ireland, yis?

- That's right.

- Nineteen eighty-eight. Are the British still there?

- They are, but we're trying to get them out.

- Good. One word of warning. Don't use radio propaganda. They'll shoot you for that. They'll shoot you and then they'll hang you.

- They don't hang you anymore. They gag you and they shoot you but they don't hang you. Not since—

- I did broadcasts from Zeesen, Hamburg and Bremen and the bastards got me.

- I don't understand.

- Shot me first and then hanged me.

- There's some mistake.

- No mistake. They hated me. I hit the British morale, you see. Scared the shit out of them.

- Lord Haw-Haw! You're Lord Haw-Haw!

- Yis. That's what they called me. Some two-bit

175

newspaper flunky gave me that name. They tried to ridicule me. They said during the war I was a music hall joke. Then when they captured me they said I was a threat. Hah!

- That would be them all right. Odious Albion.

- You don't know the half of it, Myles. You did say Myles, didn't you?

- Yeah. Myles Corrigan.

- After they shot me in forty-five they kept me locked up in a Dutch hospital while the shittyballs in Westminster played about with the Treason Act. Then they made it retrospective just so they could eliminate me.

- You couldn't be up to them. Sure in seventy-one they arrested John Hume illegally in Derry. Then they passed a law—

- Silence!

- Sorry?

- Achtung!

- Sorry.

- And the very next day they winched me out of that hospital and had me in court in London before you could say Helmut Rundfunk Smeilenluffer. What do you think of that?

- Typical.

- They knew I was American born, you see, just like your fine De Valera. So they twisted the law to say I could still be got for treason because I had a British passport.

- Ridiculous.

- Even though it was out of date.

- They haven't changed. Do you know what they did

after the—

- But I let them know. Yis, I let them know all right. I stood in the dock one day and shouted at them, "There's no justice in this court!"

- Fair play to you.

- They tried to get me for contempt. But my counsel Adolf Slade put them in their place. He pointed out that since Mister Justice Tucker hadn't yet arrived, being at that very moment caught in traffic, I was perfectly justified in drawing the court's attention to this matter.

- Very clever.

- And every morning this Horray Henry bird stood up and announced: "Rex versus William Joyce", as if we didn't know, hah, until one morning I decided I'd had enough of this nonsensical ritual and I called out: "The law is a smelly ass and Rex is a mad dog."

- Did that not get you into bother?

- Not really. No-justice Tucker found me guilty of contempt of court and I simply smiled at him and said, "What are you going to do, stupid Tucker? Hang me twice? Yis?"

- Brilliant!

- Oh I showed them up all right.

- But they got you in the end, didn't they?

- They did, the bastards.

- Listen. I hope you'll not be offended when I say this but I was actually trying to contact a James Joyce.

- Ah. That'll be my Uncle Jimbo from Mayo. Place called Ballinrobe. Do you know it?

- Let me think. I think I may have passed through it once.

- You're not in agriculture, are you?

- I'm not, actually. Though I do own a field in Donegal.

- Uncle Jimbo was in agriculture but only in a small way, you understand. Aunt Biddy used to say sometimes, "I don't know the last time I tasted a bit of meat" and Jimbo would always say back to her, "Well now, let's see if we can't rustle you up a nice piece of mutton". So then he'd go out and pick a good burly sheep for her from up the hill behind one of the big houses."

- Ah, the big houses.

- Yis. You know those places supposedly belonging to the Anglo-Irish goofs. The chinless wonders of the western world.

- Right. Got you.

- Yis indeed. Jimbo always reckoned he might as well have a sheep as a lamb. By the way, it was very good of you to try and contact him. I'll tell him you called.

- I'd really love to get talking to him sometime but it's ... actually James Joyce the writer I wanted to speak to.

- Oh, that Jew-lover. He's the man who wrote a ton weight of gibberish about a day in the life of some impotent Jew called Penfold Broom that wanders around Dublin, isn't he? *Ulysses* I think he called it. *Useless* would have been more like it. Hah! Anyway, you should have told me before now. I've been wasting my time with you. Try another wavelength. Goodbye. Victory to the fatherland!

- Ah ....

- Up the blackshirts!

- James Joyce?

- Yes.

- James Augustine Joyce?

- Yes yes. What is it?

- Formerly of Dublin, Bray, Pola, Paris, Trieste, Zürich, Amsterdam and Rome?

- You're not getting a penny! I'm dead!

- What?

- You're too late. I passed on ages ago. I'm a shade, do you hear, a shade!

- Please. I'm not—

- Talk to Stephen. He'll see to you. He's my grandson. He'll soon sort you out.

- You don't understand. I'm not looking for money.

- What?

- You don't owe me anything.

- Thank the lord Finnegan for that. I thought for a minute there you were one of the posse from the Pale.

- I'm sorry to have given you such a start. Look, can I get straight to the point? Time is of the essence here.

- Of course. Proceed.

- My name is Myles Corrigan. I'm the central character in a flawed but brilliantly original novel set in Northern Ireland. Only it's not finished yet and the author's down with writer's block and is threatening to kill me. He's gaga so he is.

- I wouldn't be too concerned about that. Very common complaint among writers. And dying can often work to your advantage. Did you know that? You have to die to become immortal. Who ever heard of a living person being immortal?

- I understand what you mean but he's also saying that he's going to burn the manuscript if he can't come up with an inconclusive ending by tomorrow.

- Jesus! Don't let him do that. I threw a manuscript in the fire one time and it took blood, sweat and I don't know how many quarts of Jameson's finest to put those people together again. Jesus pleaseus! Who is this arsehole anyway?

- Colm Herron.

- Never heard of him.

- He's after your time.

- What are you talking about! There's no such thing. And just because someone's dead doesn't mean he stops reading. I've virtually read everything of any significance since I got here in forty-one and I've never come across this bird. Hollom Cairn? Never heard of him.

- Colm Herron.

- No, it doesn't register. I'm actually into the postmodern subconciousness thing. He wouldn't know anything about that.

- I think maybe he does.

- I don't believe it. I'm in touch, you see. You have to keep up with the bastards to stay ahead of them. Here, what do you think of this? I did it this morning. It's my ninety-first draft in forty-seven years. Would you like to hear it?

- I'd love to.

- This is Majella Mirabelle Lilypond, granddaughter of Molly Bloom stemming from Molly's never-before-mentioned liaison with a Kerry cockle-picker called Winklehurst Broad. Majella lies half awake blinking this thought about someone and, of course, she's barely aware of it:

Come my slave my master my blackguard-boy my big fucking
man-whore. Come here again like the time we had at Howth.
It flits on me it fleets and flits on me how we capered at
the rain-drenched hedge like a sow and her mate
clabbered in each other's stink and sweat.
O I remember I remember when you threw me down and
said You're mine and that time
the time the gulls were nearly landing on us
you were like a soft big tulipbud all sweet and wet
till you shouted Now! Now! and the sepals folded
back and the petals opened wide just so quick and you
gorged me with your milky dew O yes and you let this
big groan out of you that you'd have thought you
were going to die or something and that's the time
that's the time you cried and said you loved me.

- Oh my God! It's wonderful!

- I just gave you that passage for fear you wouldn't like the less sensual bits.

- Oh no. I love everything you do. I live you. You're deep down in me.

- Hold on. Just taking a mental note here. Live-you.- Deep-down-in-me. Listen. You may be the very one I've been waiting for to type up this book. It's as ready as it's ever going to be. I have to get it out of here.

- Onto the shelves?

- Onto the earth. I'm rather disadvantaged, you see. It's so bloody hard to get a secretary in this place. Tell me, which medium are you using to contact me?

- EVP.

- Never heard of them. Willie Butler Yeats was into this sort of thing. Did you ever come across him? Bit of a poet.

- Oh yeah, of course I have. He won the Nobel prize for literature, didn't he?

- He did. Farce. The only thing nobel about that crowd is their name. Should be blown up the whole lot of them. Anyway, tell me more about these EVP people.

- It's not people. It's a form of technology. It stands for electronic voice phenomenon. You do it yourself.

- Remarkable. You're a scientist then?

- I'm not, actually. All you need for this is a rudimentary knowledge of electronics. And belief. You must believe in it. I've found that if you don't have conviction it doesn't work.

- Really? Willie's medium had several convictions. Two for fraud and five for deception, I think. Madam Gregory her name was. Had this big sign on the door as I remember: CELTIC TWILIGHT ENTERPRISES. HERE BE GHOSTS AND GOBLINS. But enough of this tittle tattle. I've been trying to find a decent secretary for nearly fifty years. Used to have one the name of Beckett but he didn't last. I was wondering maybe if you....

- Oh thank you! I'd be honoured! But how can you get the manuscript to me?

- There is no manuscript. It's in my head. I'd have to dictate it to you.

- How many words about?

- Let me see. I've got it down to just under three million, I think.

- Three million? What size of a book would that be?

- Oh I don't know. Seven thousand pages give or take a few hundred?

- Could I get back to you on this?

- Do I detect a strategic withdrawal here? I remember the time that man Beckett—

- Oh no. It's just that I won't be able to help you if I don't exist. I told you. I'm on the verge of being nullified. Once the script hits the fire I'm finished. No past, no present, no future.

- Sounds like an interesting idea. I was thinking actually for my next book I'd deal with someone who always remains the same even though he isn't there.

- That's brilliant but—

- It's a development, you see. *Finnegans Wake* was about night and the dream-state. The one you're going to type up is about that passing intimation that jiggles in and out between the unconscious and the semiconscious and the subconscious and the conscious.

- Got you.

- You know how thousands of mornings in bed might pass and then this particular nanosecond the feeling flashes that you (and I say you merely by way of hypothesis) don't really want the person you've been lying beside for years. Or perhaps you understand for the first time that all human existence is futile and life and death have no meaning so why get up?

- If I could just—

- And this next book, you see, will be the last in the trilogy which started with *Finnegans Wake*. The opening passage will have just the one word in it—

- Look, I have to—

- written four hundred and sixty-four times.

- You're serious? What word?

- I was thinking of nun. Or Navan. Possibly Navan. Any word that's the same spelt backwards. Tit would be good. Lately I've been coming round to tit. It's what they call a palindrome.

- Ah.

- But enough about me. The most immediate concern is to keep you going. Tell me something. Have you ever written anything creative?

- Well, in a previous draft of the novel I'm in I was in the process—

- Because I was thinking you could perhaps finish the book for this man Cairn. A little clever persuasion is all that would be needed.

- You think so?

- I know so. What was it you wrote, anyway?

- In a recent draft of Colm Herron's book I'd got to near the end of a novel when the British troops raided my flat.

- Still at it are they?

- Yeah. They kicked my head in and when I got back to the flat after five weeks in hospital I found most of my manuscript scattered on the floor with soldiers' boot tracks all over it.

- There's your book!

- I know. I realised almost right away. It worked out well, actually, because I wasn't happy with the thing I'd been writing.

- What subject were you dealing with?

- Twenty-four hours in the life of Edward Badran, a Palestinian asylum seeker who hasn't had proper sex with his wife for years. He's a man who's taken a few knocks, he's on a bad run and he's just trying to get through the day, you see. The novel was supposed to be a kind of protest against the vulgarity of military heroism and the stupid machismo of sexual prowess.

- Hm. Had you a name for it?

- Yeah. *Hercules*. This guy wanders about Derry the whole book thinking away into himself and chatting to people and doing all these very ordinary things but he's actually based on the mythical Greek hero.

- Sounds okay to me.

- Do you really think so? I had the feeling it somehow lacked the *depth* a work of art needs.

- I'm beginning to like you, Myles. I've always thought of life as the River Liffey, if you know what I mean, and one day a book that's heavy and substantial lands on it and sinks to the bottom and another book that's light and slight and shiny is at the same time being carried along by a little wave and it bobbles about the surface and people are queued up on the banks and the bridges to catch a glimpse of it so that they can tell other people they've seen it and then a different wave comes along and the bauble is gone as quickly as it came. And, as we know, the book on the bed of the river lies waiting to be discovered by those few who are prepared to explore the deep.

- That's exactly what I thought, James. My new book was going to be incomprehensible to nearly everybody.

- Good man yourself. Keep them guessing. That's what I always say.

- Yeah. It was this really obscure allegory of how the state and the Church give their approval to those who conform and stamp on those who question and challenge. Imprimatur. Imprint. Get it?

- You're certainly onto something there, Myles.

- I was onto something except Colm Herron threw it out in his third draft. All I am now is a sad drunken clown who can't even get it up. And as if things aren't bad enough, I'm also on the brink of annihilation.

- Look, I may be able to help you with that. The annihilation thing.

- You're really serious about this?

- It depends on your powers of persuasion. But you'll have to promise me, Myles, that once you're safe you'll get my new work out on the market.

186

- Front of the store, James. Front table of every bookshop in town. You have my word.

- In town? I'm talking about the world, Myles. For a start you've got to get me into China. China is the future.

- No problem.

- Good. Now listen. You're going to have to persuade Hollom Cairn to let you finish his book.

- No chance. He'd never agree.

- I think he just might. He knows all about your writing potential. Tell him he'll be given full credit for the novel. Just ask in return that your name appears in his dedication on page five or wherever he puts it. You know, instead of *To my dear wife Griselda* or *To Tess, my loving secret whore* or whatever sort of nonsense he was planning. Tell him the alternative would be for him to be drugged to death. He's already gaga, isn't he? Has he been committed yet?

- He has.

- I thought as much. There you are. You've got him by the bollocks. Be blunt. Say to him, "Hollom, the choice is yours. Would you rather be read or dead?"

- I still don't think he'll do it.

- All right. Let me ask you one more question then. What's his opinion of me?

- He adores you.

- Good. Tell him that after spending twelve years at *Finnegans Wake* I asked a man called James Stephens to agree to finish it in the event of my becoming ill or dead.

- I've heard of him. He's supposed to be very good. Didn't he write *The Crock of Gold*?

- He did. Load of crap so it was. No, the reason I liked him was his name and his time of birth.

- I don't understand.

- His name is a combination of mine and that of the hero of my first novel.

- Stephen Dedalus!

- Yes. And James Stephens was born at six o'clock on the morning of the second of February, eighteen eighty-two.

- The same time as you!

- Exactly.

- A twin soul.

- Indeed. Now, tell all that to this man Cairn. Pretend to him that I told you Stephens actually completed my novel. Tell him he can check it out with me on EVP if he wishes. With the right kind of persuasion you're onto a winner, Myles.

- My God! I think I can do it!

- Of course you can. Cairn needs closure on this one. Give him closure. Give him the most inconclusive ending in the history of literature.

- I can do it!

- The future beckons, Myles. For you and for me.

- I'm going to do it!

- Go, Myles, go!

- Now, if you'd just read out that first bit.

- Right. Clause one of two: I, Colm Herron, agree that

Myles Corrigan should write the conclusion of my novel *Further Adventures of James Joyce* provided I am named as sole author.

- Okay? Everything okay there?

- I'm not too happy with the word conclusion, Myles. Do you think we could change it to inconclusion?

- Absolutely, Colm. That's no problem at all. Look. There. It's changed. See?

- Yes. Very good. Now listen. I'm depending on you to get this right. No soft focus. No rose tints. I don't want Conn riding off into the sunset. I want him walking out of a post office, or a supermarket possibly, listening to some mindgrinding bore talking to him about the weather. Or sitting in a traffic jam thinking it's maybe time he changed the air freshener. You know, the one that's always shaped like a Christmas tree. Or trying to remember exactly what it was that started his bleeding piles.

- Consider it done.

- Loose ends everywhere. Realism, Myles. Realism. Remember, *Finnegans Wake* ended in the middle of a sentence.

- With the word the. Isn't that right?

- Yes. Now, my book must end with the word and. I need people to turn over the page expecting to read more. You'll be able to do this, won't you?

- Of course.

- And you, Myles. You're the stuff of pathos. A complete loser. I appreciate that you don't want to die. That's understandable, nobody wants to die. But if you must save yourself make sure and save yourself for more heavy drinking and the slow descent into heart disease and liver failure.

- I like it!

- This is *art* you're at, not rainbows. Right?

- Check. Now, would you mind calling out the other part, Colm? Just to see if you're happy with it.

- Okay. Clause two of two: I further agree that my dedication on page five should now read: *To the real Myles Corrigan without whom this novel would never have been completed.*

- Sounds perfect. Doesn't it?

- I don't know, Myles. There may be some readers who'll suspect that you *literally* finished the book for me.

- Not at all. That's too fantastic for words. I mean, nobody in their right mind could possibly believe that.

- You think not?

- I know not.

- What?

- Listen, Colm. I really need to get moving here. Your agent has to have the manuscript in six weeks' time.

- He's a bastard, Myles. Did I tell you that?

- You did. And I agree. Big, big bastard. But he's under pressure, Colm. He wants to get the thing out there in time to enter it for this year's Booker prize.

- That's exactly what I'm talking about. Do you realise who the chairman of the Booker judging panel is?

- Who?

- Morgan Cleethorpes.

- Oh yeah, that's right. He's the man who ran the four-minute mile last summer, isn't he?

- Right. The millionth person to have done it. That's his claim to fame, Myles. I mean, what the fuck's happening? He's only ever read two books in his life. *How to run the Four-minute Mile* by Roger Bannister or somebody. And what was the other one?

- *How to run a Mile in under Four Minutes* by Chris Chataway.

- And there he is on Channel Four presenting the hit series about the Egyptian pyramids.

- He's a big celebrity. You have to admit that, Colm. He's a household name.

- So's Jeyes fluid. So's Dulcolax laxatives. So's—

- Steady on now.

- It's enough to send you mental. You know, of course, that if it hadn't been for that talk I had with James I'd never have agreed to all this.

- But isn't it great! Imagine! You're James Joyce and I'm James Stephens! J J and S. It's like John Jameson and Son.

- Sons.

- Son.

- Sons.

- Whatever. I must go, Colm. Deadlines.

- You won't forget about the style?

- Style?

- Yes. I told you, remember? Don't change it one iota. Everything you do must be in my individual style. No one, but no one, must be able to spot the join.

- Of course, Colm. Just leave it to me. Now, if you wouldn't mind writing your name here at the bottom of this sheet.

A PAINFUL CASE

*The waiting cock gets ready to have its way. So what will
the pretty hens do about that then?*

They met at the Waterfoot Inn. He knew her as soon as she
walked in, even before she smiled and waved at him. He saw
relief on her face at the same moment as he took in her full
firm body. She was wearing a white blouse and tight-fitting
blue jeans that brought a rush of anticipation to his senses.
He went forward and as he kissed her on the cheek he held
the fingers of her right hand in the cup of his left.

 - You're welcome, he said and smiled, staying close to her
for a few seconds. Just before they separated her lips touched
the tip of his chin and she found her voice.

 - Thanks. I was afraid you wouldn't come.

 - Why would I do that? he said.

She was almost beautiful, with the face of a woman and
the light walk of a girl. Her hair was a rich auburn now and
the waves of it fell to below her shoulders. The high
cheekbones were more prominent than he remembered and

the gaze of her blue eyes was softer, less sure than it used to be.

He led her to a low table and stood while she settled for the seat across from his glass of wine.

- What'll you have? he asked.

- Same as you. Whatever you're drinkin.

He went to the bar. She opened her handbag and took out a tiny mirror. Peeping anxiously into it she ran her tongue around her lips and patted the front of her hair. While she did this she glanced up twice to see where he was. The second time she looked her eyes lingered for an extra few moments and her heart seemed to turn over on its side at the nearness of him. When he came back they spoke together.

- Blossom Hill okay? White?

- This is a very nice place, isn't it?

She glanced at the wine. - Anythin at all. Thanks.

She looked vaguely to right and left. - I was here once before and it didn't seem as nice. Blossom Hill's fine. I'm no connoisseur.

- Would you believe it? he said. - I've only been here twice myself.

- Is that right?

He's better than I dreamed. Oh God help me get this right.

- Aye. Not many people from the cityside come here as far as I know.

- Right enough?

- Not many, he said again.

She looked at some of the faces near her and he followed the path of her eyes without taking in what he saw.

- I don't know one person here, he said.

194

- Except for me.

He smiled. - Except for you. What about the conference? How's it goin?

- It doesn't begin till tomorrow. I came today so I wouldn't be drivin down in a hurry in the mornin.

- I thought it started today. Where's it on?

- The Everglades.

She gave him a sudden admiring look and said - You've aged well, Conn. I can't get over it.

Her voice began to race ahead of her. - You're really distinguished-lookin. Thirty years. Imagine.

He lowered his eyes for a few moments and when he raised them he stared across at her and said - It's a long time.

- I was just thinkin—

- You're lovely. You're still lovely, he said.

She blushed happily. - You should see me in the mornins.

She laughed and the rising red on her cheeks spread quickly to the rest of her face.

- How's James? he asked and saw immediately from her expression that she didn't like the question. But he went on. - I haven't seen him since... I don't know... it must be nineteen sixty-one.

- James is fine, she said. - James Sinico hasn't a care in the world.

- Where's he teachin?

- The two of us have been livin apart for years. In the same house. Do you know what I mean?

He nodded without understanding. She spoke even faster than before. - It can be done, you know. You're busy with your

195

work and your children and their education and the years go on. You just don't see how you can do the right thing.

- You were sayin on the phone.

- I knew nearly from the start but then there were the children one after the other. I was stupid. Another Irish martyr, I suppose.

She gave a little laugh, then sighed and went silent. After a minute she half-closed her eyes and said - Do you remember who was it that wrote about isolation and all that sort of thing?

He didn't answer.

- Do you not remember, Conn? He was on our English course in Belfast. You did him too. He was always writin about it. I think he called it the incurable loneliness of the human condition.

- I don't know.

- I joined the Charismatic movement away back. And then Cursillo. Would you believe that?

She gazed wide-eyed at him with a mixture of bemusement and embarrassment.

- Can you see me in those? she asked. - Can you?

He shook his head.

- met a lot of lonely people, she said. - You wouldn't believe it. It's like...you know, the Beatles' song. What one is it?

- *Eleanor Rigby.*

- That's it. All the lonely people.

She gave a tight smile. - Religion was good for me, she said. - It got me through.

She looked at him intently as if it was she who was doing the listening.

- You've finished that drink, said Conn. - Here.

He called over a waiter, a thin pimply teenager with a shaven head.

- Could we have two white Blossom Hills, please?

- Yes sir.

- And tell me. What time do you serve dinner here?

- Six o'clock tell eight thirty.

Conn looked at his watch.

- Have you a menu?

- Yes sir. I'll bring it over now.

The boy went away.

- I'm starved with hunger, said Lucia. - And my head's light too. I shouldn't be drinkin on an empty stomach.

She half rose. - Excuse me a minute. Must go and powder my nose. Don't go away.

He watched her as she walked to the ladies'. All those years ago he'd never dared look at her the way he looked now. Then she had touched his soul. And that was the height of it, he thought. That was about all she got touching. Just before she went out of sight he saw a little lift of one of her shoulders that took him by surprise and brought a memory he didn't want. They were running hand in hand in Falls Park. She pretended to stumble and then she fell to the grass behind some bushes, pulling him in on top of her. *You meant more to me than I did to myself and you blighted me. You demanded what I wasn't ready to do. You teased and tormented and I wasn't ready. But you couldn't wait. You blighted me. Between*

197

you and religion I hadn't a chance. And now. Now you're afraid to ask. Would you not like to know? Will I tell you? The craving for your company, even for the sight of you, the knowing that you'd given yourself to a strutting cock, the sleeplessness, then the not believing, the makebelieving, the breakdown, the shock of the electric shocks. Will I tell you? The pitiable plans for suicide. Half in love with easeful death but more in fear of hell. I loved you with a love you wouldn't understand and there you were, naked in some borrowed weekend bed under that bastard. Do you want to know about loneliness? Will I tell you?

The glare of a late-spring sunset flashed from the river and two waitresses hurried to close the drapes. A discreet glow of concealed lighting now covered the dining room and the softly-piped music had begun to fill her with waves of longing. She reached a hand across the table to him and he held it.

- I took all your wine, she said, giggling a little.

- No, I got plenty.

- You did not. I drank the whole bottle nearly.

She stroked his palm with her first and second fingers. - Anyway, it was a lovely dinner, she said. - You know how to treat a lady, Conn. What does the song say?

- I'm not sure. What song is that?

She wrinkled her forehead for a few moments and then said - It doesn't matter. Some old one.

In the elevator she leaned her head on his shoulder and held him tightly around the waist with both arms.

- Kiss me, she said.

The door slid open and he smiled down at her.

- Come on, he said. - This is us.

He looked at the key. - One one nine. Why do they do that? Everybody knows they haven't a hundred and nineteen rooms. Let me see. Where are we?

- Mister and Missus Conn Doherty, she said in a low voice of mock secrecy. As they walked along the carpeted corridor she took his arm and held it against the side of her warm breast. - When you signed that register I'm sure I must have blushed to the roots. There was me thinkin, If those ones in Downpatrick could see me now.

He smiled. - All the hallelujah ones. They'd never let you back. Here we are.

He unlocked the door and pushed it open.

- There's my suitcase, she said, surprised.

- Of course it's your suitcase. Do you not remember me gettin the waiter to bring it up?

- Oh, Conn, I think I'm drunk. I forgot all about it.

When the door closed behind them she came close to him and put her arms around his neck.

- Would you kiss me? she said.

He drew her against him and kissed her hard on the mouth. Almost immediately she began to loosen his belt and after some clumsiness managed to get his trousers down around his ankles. She dropped to her knees and tugged at his underpants. His penis sprang briefly to attention and then fell against her face. A solitary bead of pale fluid perched on the tip like a small almond. She kissed it off and another one immediately replaced it.

- Lucia, he said.

She didn't answer. He heard her quick urgent breath as she held his half-erection in both hands and brought her mouth down over the faintly malodorous smell of it. Then her fingers moved to behind him.

- Lucia, he said.

She was inflamed now, pulling at him as if wanting to tear him apart. To stem the surge of semen he pressed his palms into the crown of her head until she let him slip from her mouth and cried for him to stop. When he did she took her fingers from him and lowered her hands. She looked tearfully up at him.

- I'm sorry, he said, - but I'd have nothin to give.

She got to her feet a little unsteadily and kissed him on the lips.

- I haven't even started, she said and tried to smile. She rubbed her cheeks with the sides of her hands and sniffed. A little watery bubble disappeared up one of her nostrils.

- I'm just goin into the shower, she said. - I'll be no time at all.

She kissed him again and then stood back, searching his eyes. After she left him he looked down in approval at his penis, now standing straight as an arrow. Then he stripped to the skin and got into bed.

When she came to him she was wearing only a short pink nightdress. He slid it smoothly over her head and tossed it on the floor. He caressed her breasts and kissed the nipples of them and the soft smell of her jasmine brought him to a

200

higher state of readiness. They lay side by side and held each other tightly. Suddenly she shuddered, rocking against him so hard that he was afraid he was going to ejaculate. He pushed her away from him and said - What's wrong?

She gave a weak little cry and then began to wail.

- Hold me, Conn. Hold me.

He held her but not as closely as before. He felt himself go slowly limp and an irritation grew in him. Then the wailing stopped.

- Tell me what's wrong, he said.

- I should be so happy, Conn. I've wanted this for so long and I....

She let out a piteous sob.

- What?

- I'm so sorry for what I did to you. It was a terrible thing I did.

- Don't think about it. It's all right.

- I knew you needed time. I knew I should have been patient. I didn't have the sense. I've dreamed about us for so long.

- You didn't come to visit me.

- What?

- You didn't come to visit me.

She began to tremble violently and he heard a low moan.

- I was scared of Gransha, Conn, she whispered. - I was so frightened at the thought of it. The things you used to hear.

- I was there for four and a half months.

- I didn't want you to be holdin out hope. I thought you'd come round quicker if you didn't see me.

- I saw you all right. When I came out I saw you with him every day.

- I never stopped lovin you, Conn. I was only married a year and I knew. I woke up one mornin and I knew.

She came against him again and clung to him. He flinched, trying to hold his seed in check.

- Oh Conn, Conn. Please forgive me. Can you forgive me? Do you love me?

- I love you. Would you turn over for me?

- I've never been with anyone else. There was only you. The number of times I wanted to ring you. But my faith wouldn't allow me. I was stupid.

- Turn over for me, would you?

- When I rang you last week it was like wakin from a long sleep. Why did I never have the courage before? Why do you want me to turn over? What are you doin?

- Just lie on your stomach. Please.

- What's that you have in your hand? Let me see it.

- It's just a little tube of gel.

- Oh Conn, no. Please.

- Do you love me? You said you loved me.

- I do. I love you. Don't do this. I don't like this. Please.

He rolled her body over and pulled the bedclothes away.

- You wouldn't deny me this, would you, Lucia? I've never forgotten you. I need you this way.

She gave a soft whimper.

- I've problems there, Conn. Since the children. Please.

- It'll be all right. It'll be all right with the gel. Relax.

- Please. Please.

- I can't wait, Lucia. It'll all be gone on me. Now lie still.

She didn't come down to breakfast. He was happy about that because without her he was able to enjoy his bacon, egg and sausages in peace. For three months this had been the difficulty with Melanie. No matter how good the Saturday morning lovemaking was he still missed the old peace and pleasure of sitting alone with his fry and his Irish Times.

He asked a waiter to bring more bacon and while he waited he read some of the preview of the Wembley cup final. The bacon arrived crisp and hot and when he had finished eating it he turned to the Arts section. He scanned it and then glanced up automatically. Some people just arriving in the dining room had stopped to speak to a man and woman seated at a table close to his. The loud vulgar voices from both parties irritated him. However, along with the couple standing was a pretty girl with frizzy red hair and Conn found it difficult to take his eyes off her. She stood, hands in pockets, shifting impatiently from foot to foot and he couldn't help noticing that her chest was braless. This was obvious because the nipples of her partly formed breasts were prominent on her white T-shirt. She also wore a pair of frayed blue jeans that hung from her hips and clung to her lower stomach and inner thighs. He noted with pleasure the spoiled insolent look about her freckled face. After a minute she took one hand from her pocket and pulled at her T-shirt, then slowly stroked the swell of her little white belly.

Ah. What age would she be? Fourteen? Fifteen? I wonder if she shaves it. She's been about this one, I'd say. Fifteen maybe. Hard to know. They're so advanced now they could teach you plenty.

Over the top of his propped-up newspaper he viewed her intently. He was able to see as far down as her knees while still appearing to read. A long silent baconfed fuck.

I would buy you lace. Black? You like black? And an emerald tiara for your hair. Dance for me. Dance for me tonight.

She moved almost rhythmically from one foot to the other and he went on watching until her eyes lit boldly on his. Thrilled and confused he turned his head quickly to the right as if looking for someone he knew. He felt the caress of her clothes and the heat of her breath and her skin.

Is it possible?

His eyes returned to the Irish Times. NIETZSCHE: THE MAN WHO INVENTED SUPERMAN BEFORE THE COMIC STRIP OR HOLLYWOOD WERE HEARD OF. The grating voices of the girl's company continued. He raised his eyes. Her father, cheery, ruddy and fat, was looking vacantly in Conn's direction. BUT NIETZSCHE'S SUPERMAN WAS FRIENDLESS AND ALONE, ARROGANT AND SUPERB.

Must read that. Wouldn't mind reading that later. I'd say she's looking at me. Little vixen.

The father turned back to the two that were seated and laughed loudly. Then he half-circled the table and leaned over the shoulder of the other man, trying to tell him something and almost choking with laughter.

- And the best of it was, he said and then fell into a paroxysm of mirth. The girl was moving from side to side, now facing Conn full on, her fingers still carelessly fondling her belly.

Is she smiling? Was that a smile? Soft flesh yielding, body arched, rumpled bedclothes, the sweet private scent of her sweat.

Their eyes met again and the breath stopped in his throat. Oops. *Ahhh. That's all right. Ahhh. No harm done. What do you know? Didn't think I'd any left after this morning.*

The conversation ended abruptly and the three walked towards Conn. Senses jolted, he looked down at the newspaper and then up. Still smiling from their encounter the couple nodded amiably as they walked past him. Trailing behind was the girl. She didn't seem aware of him but the pale fingers of her left hand stole quickly along the rim of the table close to his elbow. She and her parents sat directly behind him and he heard her speak.

- I'm starved, she said. - Can I get two eggs?

Her voice was coarse but the pleading in it brought fresh titillation. His body gave one last late beat of delight and he gazed unseeing at the propped-up Arts section. He sat on for awhile making the most of the glow inside him, then folded the newspaper and got up. When he reached the door of the dining room he turned and glanced back. Her eyes were down and her mouth was crammed with food. The only sound from her table was the clink of delph on delph.

He went to the bedroom. She wasn't there. He called her name but there was no answer. The bed had been neatly made and the windows were wide open. He stood looking around, not knowing why. His eyes fell on the bed again, on the plumped up pillows and the smooth surface of the bedspread and it almost seemed to him that nothing had happened. He repeated her name and thought he sensed the faint smell of jasmine. He saw her spread-eagled legs and soft buttocks and then for the first time he became aware of the rumble of traffic, the clash of gears and a bell tolling slowly from across the river. He went out into the corridor where he had last walked with her. She would get through the next two days of union business and then she would drive back to Downpatrick. He thought of what awaited her there and decided she didn't deserve his sympathy. She had made her bed a long time ago. Too many years had passed and too much had happened. What was not to be was never going to be. He thought with distaste of how she had so easily given herself to him, pretending she didn't want what she got and all the time using her body to try and entice him back. How that squared with her evangelical rectitude he didn't know.

He went to pay the bill.

- Room one hundred and nineteen, he said.

- One one nine, said the receptionist and then paused uncertainly. She gave a little cough and continued - Mister and Missus Doherty?

- Yes.

- Part of that bill has been paid, sir.

- What do you mean?

- Yes sir, she said pleasantly, inscrutably. - Your wife was here and paid half of it... let me think... about twenty minutes ago.

- Ah. Right, said Conn and tried to return the smile.

He wrote a cheque for the balance and then walked to the dining room. She wasn't there. Neither was *she*. The parents were gone too. He went to the front steps of the hotel and looked around outside. The redhead stood behind a cream Rover while her father loaded suitcases into the boot. She seemed smaller and younger than before and the sight of her sent a weak flutter through him. The car boot slammed shut. *Tyrone registration. Donnelly's of Dungannon. Quite a way.* She dived excitedly onto the back seat and within a minute they were out of the car park and waiting for traffic to pass on the Caw roundabout. He tried to get a last look at her but all he could see in the back windscreen was the blue sky. Two long lorries trundled close together like a great caterpillar and then the Rover moved slowly in behind them.

Conn weaved his way self-consciously along William Street. He knew he shouldn't have taken the large brandy on top of everything else but it had been a good day at the bookies. He blinked in a moment of self-understanding. We're not robots, he thought. We're all entitled to the odd bit of indulgence. When a man rakes in a hundred and eighty-five quid and his favourite team wins the English cup final, well....

The daylight troubled him. It had hit him the moment he left The Drunken Dog and it had been troubling him since. For nearly thirty years he'd been stepping out of there under cover of darkness and had never thought twice about the occasional stumble. But now it seemed to him that the sun was a spotlight and his journey home a one-man show. He shook his head disgustedly at the inequity of the world. Bishops could get pissed in their palaces, priests could get paralytic in their presbyteries and nobody said a word. But a teacher... a teacher only had to go on his mouth and nose once and half the parents in town were on about it. And there they were now, hauling home their Saturday shopping. He could certainly pick the day, the hour and the place. All the fucking ducks in a row.

He turned into Rossville Street with some relief and was almost immediately knocked sideways by a running boy.

- Sorry, said the boy and then added - Sorry, Mister Doherty. Are you okay, sir?

Winded and a little dizzy, Conn held onto the railings outside Pilots' Row Centre, taking a few moments to focus. An All Saints pupil. What was his name? A good lad. What was his name?

- Just watch where you're goin in future, Manus, he said, spacing his words carefully. *That's it. Manus. Funny how it can come when you think you've forgotten.*

- Do you want us to get you a taxi, sir?

This was another voice. There was another boy. Conn swivelled slowly. A bad little bastard this. What was his name?

- Not at all, Jason. I'm fine. You're Jason Dillinger, aren't you?

- Sir no.

- And you're Manus Doherty? Isn't that right?

- Sir yes.

Satisfied that he'd regained some dignity and asserted his

208

status, Conn went to move on.

- Are you sure you're okay, sir?

This was the blackguard speaking, the smirking little blackguard from...where was he from? Conn couldn't remember. But he remembered the family. All blackguards.

- Thanks. I'm fine, said Conn.

He turned away from them and walked on, slowly and rigidly now. A taxi would have been handy all right. But it wasn't on. The last thing he wanted was to go back to William Street and sizzle in a queue for a black taxi. He could just see it. He'd end up wedged in the back of one with a collection of heavy-haunched poker-faced women. He wouldn't stand a chance. They'd sit there scrutinising him with their hooded eyes and their little minds, storing away every slurred syllable, every careless movement, to pick over at their leisure. No, walking was the only way. He'd be back home soon anyway. And Melanie would have the dinner ready. Lamb chops, boiled spuds, gravy, peas and carrots. Half five, he'd said. He checked his watch. Right on schedule, without even trying. He smiled as he remembered how she hadn't been able to cook potatoes at the start. She'd thought they should be ready the moment the water began to boil. Poor Melanie. And then not long after she'd got the hang of it she'd gone and let them boil dry. But of course that had been his fault. He'd got so horny watching her peeling the shallots he'd shagged her on the spot. That was nearly three months ago and even now he could smell the memory of it. The steam, the burning, the sweat, the spunk. And the two of them at it like pistons gone amok. It was far and away the best fuck he'd ever had and that

209

included a convulsive one-night stand with the wolfwoman from Omagh. Some nights when Melanie was with Mickey he'd still jerk off energetically to try and savour again those rapturous minutes. She was a wonderful girl. She was so wonderful he was sometimes hardly able to believe his luck. But it sickened him at the same time to think that others had been at her before him and even now Mickey Scanlon had her four nights a week. The thought of it made him want to scream. This beautiful girl soiled by people that weren't worthy to lick his boots. A couple of times he'd almost been on the point of asking her to marry him— that would have put paid to Mickey boy— but the fact that she wasn't a virgin had stopped him. This whole virgin thing was a problem. Derry wasn't exactly coming down with them so what was a man to do? He blinked into the sunlight. A small hard pulse was starting in his head. He turned into Brandywell Road and puffed a little as he made his way slowly up the small incline at the end of it. He was feeling the heat of the day now and he tugged at his shirt sleeves where they clung to his armpits. He'd have a shower before dinner and then after the food had settled in him he'd be ready for her. He turned the corner into the Lone Moor Road and immediately began to breathe more easily. Not far to go. His mind went back to her hot embraces and bold lovemaking and something of a spring entered his step as he walked the final two hundred yards.

A LITTLE CLOUD

A thing of beauty is not necessarily a joy forever.

- Hell-o-o, he sang.

There was no answer.

- Mel-an-ie.

There was no answer and no smell of dinner. The headache that he'd hardly been aware of a few minutes earlier was now coiled tight behind his eyes. He knew why. All he'd eaten since breakfast in the Waterfoot was a bacon sandwich, not nearly enough to absorb the feed of drink he'd taken.

- Melanie!

He went to every room and then flopped into his armchair. Where the hell was she? He remembered her forgetfulness and pictured her standing in Dunne's Stores at that moment holding a dress up against her front and chittering to one of the assistants.

- Do you really think it's me? I don't know. I sometimes have the feeling that white isn't really me. What do you think?

He sat breathing hard and his irritation grew. After a minute he went to the phone in the hallway and dialled.

- Myles - Conn here. You haven't seen Melanie about, have you?

- Yeah. She's here, actually.

Myles' voice was quiet, guarded.

- There? In your flat?

- That's right.

- What's she doin there? She was supposed to be here. What's she doin there with you?

- She's been here since last night. She came to The Dog a bit upset and—

- What! Put her on.

There was a pause and then muffled voices.

- Put her on!

Complete silence.

- What the fuck's the matter with her? he shouted. - Put her on now!

- She says she doesn't want to speak to you.

Conn breathed hard, his head thumping. There was something about Myles' tone that he didn't like. Something measured, something rehearsed.

- What does she mean she doesn't want to speak to me?

- Listen, Conn. I think it might be better if you came over. Maybe if you come over—

- What do you mean? Tell HER to get the fuck over HERE, right NOW. Tell her I'm starvin.

- He says he's starvin, said Myles.

- What did she say? I heard her talkin there. What's she sayin?

212

- Look, I think you'd better come on over. She's very upset.

- Has she gone mad? What's the matter with her?

- We're not goin to get anywhere this way, Conn.

- What did she just say? She just said somethin.

- I'm goin to put the phone down now. Okay?

- Hold on! shouted Conn. His voice was hoarse with anger. - Just tell me this. Did you say anythin to her about where I was?

- No.

- I don't believe you.

- Well, I'm tellin you now. I didn't. Listen, I'm about to put the phone down. Right? I'll see you shortly.

Myles opened the front door and Conn brushed past him into the hallway.

- Where is she? he demanded.

- She's out in the kitchen.

Myles put his hand on Conn's arm. His brown eyes were dulled by sadness, his handsome rugged features creased with concern.

- Take it easy, he said. - She hardly slept.

Conn looked sharply at him and shook the hand from his arm. He came closer and pushed his nose up against Myles'.

- What the fuck was she doin here last night? he hissed. He smelled of bacon and booze, and fishing fleets and old wee. - If you so much as touched her I'll fucken—

The kitchen door opened and Melanie stood framed in an

213

oblong of light. White-haired and lovely-limbed she stood and a flame seemed to tremble on her face.

- My God! he cried. - What happened to your hair?

- Fuck away off, she said quietly.

She wore a short flesh-coloured muslin dress made translucent by the blinding sun that filled the room behind her. Myles eased his way around her, mumbling something about the garden, and she touched his shoulder as he passed. When the back door clicked shut behind him she shook her long powder-white hair in shuddering contempt and even in his strung-up state Conn couldn't help but take in the wonder of her.

- Fuck you, you steaming bag of shite, she whispered.

- Fuck ME? Fuck ME? Fuck YOU. What the fuck's the matter with you?

She moved forward a step and her thighs shone like ivory through the delicate cotton of her dress.

- Scummy big bastard, she said, her voice softer than the softest petal, gentler than the chimes of sleep.

Conn stared in disbelief.

- What have I done? he shouted. - Tell me what I've done!

The tip of her tongue moistened her full red lips and her eyes flashed green fire.

- Right. I'll tell you what you've done, you fuck. You've gone and screwed a woman old enough to be my granny.

- What!

- Grannyfucker!

- What!

- In the Blue Diddy!

- Where? Where did you say?

- The Blue Diddy!

(The Blue Diddy is a name given locally to the Waterfoot Inn on account of its roof boasting an attractive dome illuminated by what appears to be a sea-blue nipple but is in fact a two hundred watt bulb encased in a strong glass globe.)

- What are you talkin about? he blustered.

She came towards him out of the sunlight, her body deep with shadows, the pale sculpted beauty of her cheeks hued with a faint flush.

- I'll tell you what I'm talking about, arsehole, she murmured. - You told me you were going to a union conference in Downpatrick. Right? Well, Sybil Scanlon saw you in the Blue Diddy last night with your hands all over some geriatric.

- Sybil the slabber? Mickey's sister? You know what *she's* up to, don't you?

Melanie was very close to him now and he felt a mutinous twitching of the loins and a craving to hold her in his arms till she yielded. For it seemed to him that here was a vision sent by the gods to drive men mad.

- Shut the fuck up, she said and her voice was scarcely more than a sigh. - Sixty if she's a day. And Sybil saw the two of you sign the fucking register and go up in the fucking lift to beddy beds.

- And you believe that! Oh my God! What's happenin to me?

She stood with her body touching his, a wild angel, a thing of unutterable beauty. Then, giving him a quiet haunting look, she raised a dimpled knee and with crushing force slammed it into his goolies.

- Goodbye, she said.

A PORTRAIT OF THE ARTIST IN HIS PRIME

There is nothing new under the sun.
(Or the moon. Or the stars.)

They heard the shrill cry of the gulls before they saw them. Their white forms glided over the roof of the car like fish through air, then turned and made for the black knuckled wall of rocks across the bay. One, larger than the others, hung behind almost motionless before suddenly dropping headfirst to the sea a hundred or so feet below. They saw it slice silently into the water and saw the small circle of spray appear around the point of entry.

- What about that! exclaimed Melanie.

- It's still down there, said Myles.

They were in the car park at Knockamany Bens overlooking Laag beach. Evening was falling and a pale rose now covered the land for as far as they could see. It flickered on the waters and fell on their hands and faces and clothes and everything around them. Very soon a half-light came and the rose faded into the evening. They sat quietly still during this time, watching for the seagull to surface. But the air was tinged with more than the rose and the twilight and while they watched they both felt that something else was waiting to happen. After a little while Myles spoke.

- Did you see him come up yet? he asked.

Melanie shook her head. She was having trouble focusing on where the bird had hit the water because the place had been carried away by slate-grey restless waves. But her mind was distracted by something else too and an edginess in her manner was beginning to make him uneasy.

- What is it? he asked.

- It's Conn, she answered. - The more I think about it the weirder it gets.

Myles frowned. - I know what you mean. But things happen. People change.

- Who would have thought it? she said. - I mean, he behaved like a real moron and I was mad at the time but I can't help thinking ... I don't know ... I can't help wondering....

- This may sound very harsh, said Myles, - but maybe he needed revenge more than he needed you.

- Revenge? What do you mean?

Myles drew in his breath and then began.

- I never told you. The one he was with that night was the cause of a mental breakdown he had when he was seventeen or eighteen. She contacted him three weeks ago and wanted to start up again.

Melanie's eyes widened.

- Was her name Lucia? she asked.

218

- How did you know that?

- He mentioned her one time. But I thought he was well over her. Sure it was ages ago.

Myles didn't speak for a minute and then, choosing his words with care, he said - From the way he was goin on before he went to meet her I'd say he was holdin a very big grudge.

- And you mean to tell me he really wanted to get back at her? After all those years? That's why he met her?

- I'd say so, replied Myles. - God knows what happened that night.

She stared at him, lips moving as if to form another question. Images came to her and she gave a little gasp.

- My God, she said.

The tinted windscreen in front of them brought a darker hue to the evening. They sat watching the night come slowly and after what seemed to Myles like a long, long time, she said - Do you know this? I can hardly believe it was Conn Doherty in your flat that Saturday.

She spoke with finality now for she had decided to voice one last disturbing thought and then be rid of the memory.

- It was like he was possessed, she said.

They listened in silence to the far call of the birds and the murmur of the waves. And as darkness came down over the land and sea it occurred to them both that something dim and new had kindled the air around them. She leaned suddenly towards him and put her hand in his. She did it easily, naturally, as if this was the only way of holding on to the beauty they could no longer clearly see. And it seemed to Myles that it was, though he was scarcely able to believe what was happening.

- It's lovely, isn't it? she said.

When he dared to look at her she was smiling. She spoke again, the smile still on her lips.

- You're nothing like what Conn told me.

Disconcerted, he turned his face away and his voice came as if from a deep echoing well inside him.

- What did he tell you?

- He said you were wasting your life. A great mind drowning in whiskey. That's what he said.

Their hands were still together, resting in his lap, and he knew without looking that her eyes were holding him steadily in their gaze.

- I don't know about the great mind, he answered, trembling, - but I'd say I was goin down for the third time all right.

Her fingers moved softly and moistly in the cup of his hand.

- When did you stop? she asked him.

- Two weeks ago. The night you came to The Dog.

- And how are you coping?

I'm about to burst. Your wrist is lying across my lap and I'm about to burst.

- Okay actually. My problem was, I looked on The Dog as a kind of refuge. Only it was more like a refugee camp and I didn't want to know that. All I needed was for you to walk in the door and talk to me. I just made up my mind there and then that I wasn't goin to be the author of my own destruction.

220

She opened out his hand and pressed the palm of hers warmly on it. - Here's what I can't understand, she said. - How did you manage to do all that writing and you out drinking seven nights a week?

His answer came very quickly.

- Routine, he said. - I'd about two hours of a clear head every day and I just got on with it. It seemed to come without any bother.

She shook her head in admiration.

- I've read everything you gave me, she said. - It's brilliant. I don't think anybody else in the whole world could have written what you wrote.

- I know I've got hold of somethin.

- I think you're a genius, Myles. Those thoughts Majella has in bed just as she's waking up. How did you do it?

He lowered his eyes from her gaze.

- I've got that part off by heart, she went on. - The part where she remembers.

She screwed up her face in happy concentration and began:

Come my slave my master my blackguard-boy my big fucking
  man-whore. Come here again like in the hills above the Swilly.
It flits on me it fleets and flits on me how we capered at
  the rain-drenched hedge like a sow and her mate
  clabbered in each other's stink and sweat.
O I remember I remember when you threw me down and
  said You're mine and that time
  the time the gulls were nearly landing on us
  you were like a soft big tulipbud all sweet and wet

221

till you shouted Now! Now! and the sepals folded
back and the petals opened wide just so quick and you
gorged me with your milky dew O yes and you let this
big groan out of you that you'd have thought you
were going to die or something and that's the time
that's the time you cried and said you loved me.

Myles looked into the darkness while she recited. A bell beat faintly from the chapel at Laag and ghostly little frills of foam frolicked here and there along the bay. When she'd said the last words of the passage she seemed to sigh and then went quiet.

- I can't see you right, Myles, she said after a minute, - but I think you're blushing.

He tried to speak but stopped, not trusting himself.

- There's no call to be embarrassed about that, she went on. - It's what happens.

He knew then what was coming and could almost hear the words before she said them.

- Can we go into the back?

He felt his head nodding and as he stepped from the car onto the tarmac his legs began to buckle. But he gripped the top of the door with both hands and was able to stand upright. She stood looking across the roof at him, confident, coaxing, reassuring.

- All right? she said.

She was younger than the child he'd never had and she was taking him along, showing him the way.

- All right, he said.

He made it to the back seat and she slid from the other

end till she was beside him. He touched her forehead with his fingers and then she kissed him on the lips and he felt as if his heart had been blown wide open.

- Here, she said suddenly, pulling away. - Just let me do this.

She undressed him quickly and efficiently with light little comments about zips and buckles and buttons. Then she pushed him back and he lay waiting, breathless, his body in uproar.

- Hold on, she said.

She stripped without embarrassment and a sharp sweetness came down on him. She put her face to his stomach and the uproar grew to a riot as the long waves of her hair cascaded over his nakedness. Soon she lowered herself onto him and they lay rocking, jockeying with one accord. Suddenly, easily, he entered her and let loose a cry, profane, delirious, disbelieving. His outburst disturbed a flock of sleeping sheep and the air was immediately filled with frightened angry bleatings. Myles wept with the release of a long-pent-up love and presently his cries turned to sighs as his blood slowed and the last of his seed left him. All this time she had lain compliant and calm, whispering encouragement, but now she began to writhe on him and he heard her breathing quicken. Gratefully, jubilantly, he held her hard against him, caressing her where he could, kissing her where he could as her spasms shook them both. They were alone together under the vast dark dome where the stars and planets moved and turned. The only sounds they could hear outside of themselves were the fading bleats from the field and the whisper and suck of the water on the shingle and sand. He tasted the sweetness from her and felt her body soft in his and wished this time would last forever.

EXILES
(Act One)

I go to encounter for the millionth time the reality of experience and to forge in the smithy of my soul the uncreated conscience of my race.

A Portrait of the Artist as a Young Man
James Joyce

Myles had been wanting to get away from Derry and The Drunken Dog for years and when he finally made the break it was Melanie who gave him the kick-start he needed. Three weeks after their get-together at Knockamany Bens they rented a bungalow in the little village of Muff just over the border in Donegal. Myles had hoped to leave the island of Ireland and travel widely in Europe with his lover as James Joyce had done eighty years before in the company of Nora Barnacle. However, this wasn't on what with Myles' fear of flying and the thing he had about seasickness. So he and Melanie motored to Muff where they made their home five miles from Derry and a hundred yards inside the Republic of Ireland.

Short and all as this journey was Myles felt satisfied that he'd crossed an important frontier and kept telling himself and Melanie that, while Muff wasn't exactly Paris, it wasn't Derry either. To celebrate his escape he decided to call their new home *Dedalus* after the mythical Greek inventor who made wax wings for flight. And now that he'd followed at least part of the way in Joyce's footsteps he went about continuing the odyssey by processing the remainder of his masterpiece. In a soundproofed room at *Dedalus* he spent eight hours each day for the next four years installed with his beloved computer, radio and tape recorder.

Now as any great writer will tell you, the most difficult part of perfecting a work of art is knowing what to leave out and it took Myles another five years to cut the seven thousand pages of his magnum opus to just under six hundred.

The novel was published amid rows and ructions. On one of his fortnightly visits to Derry to collect his giros for disability living allowance and incapacity benefit Myles had persuaded the editor of the Londonderry Sentinel to feature some racy bits of the book in that newspaper. This was essentially a pilot scheme designed to enrage the righteous and engage the filthy-minded and by so doing get people to ask questions they'd never asked before. And it worked. By the time the book came out seven excerpts had appeared in the Sentinel and half of Derry was enquiring about Myles' whereabouts with a view to dismembering him while many of the other half were wondering whether it was really possible to assume those kinds of positions without dislocating their spines. What inflamed the Myles seekers as much as anything else was the fact that these hundreds of column inches of "titillating tripe", as the Derry Journal described them, were appearing in a Protestant newspaper which was now being read by tens of thousands of Catholics.

But Ireland is a place of island universes and this storm in a northern teacup brought not a ripple to the rest of the country. And then John McGahern stepped in. The great Irish writer penned a glowing review of Myles' novel in the Irish Times and thus set in motion an interesting chain of events. (McGahern was still remembered by the Catholic hierarchy, of course, as the malevolent midwife [or more often the demon doctor] who had several times delivered large litters of kittens in parochial houses and bishops' palaces throughout the land.) As current after current of hot air rose ugly clouds and fierce gales began to gather all along the Irish seaboard and a consensus grew among senior churchmen and the literati that McGahern had finally blown his last remaining chances of picking up a papal knighthood. And yet, as sometimes happens in these types of cases, there was a silver lining. For the review turned out to be the trigger that shot Myles to the top of the bestseller lists, first in Ireland, then in Britain and, most remarkably of all, in China.

The book, however, stayed stubbornly unsold in the U S of A for some time as Christian, Islamic and Jewish evangelicals combined to keep it out. It wasn't, in fact, until a budding young American writer by the name of David Eggers wrote a feature for the New Yorker in which he described the novel as "a heartbreaking work of galloping genius" that the difficulty was overcome. Within a short time Myles' creation had scaled the north face of moral America's embargo, strutted on its summit and rolled head over heels and knickerless down the other side.

Such was Myles' notoriety now that the Catholic bishops of Ireland felt compelled to comment. They met at Maynooth College and promptly pronounced the book pornographic. One of the group even went so far as to tell the journalists assembled outside that he wouldn't read it even if each of them were to hand him a hundred pounds there and then. However, another bishop suddenly stalked away from the rest and the newsmen followed him, scenting a good story. Doctor Oswald Oddie, or Ozzie Oddie as he was sometimes known in press circles, was a great rambling hulk of a man who had never much cared what people thought about him. He had been looked on during his earlier ministry as something of a loose canon but had still made it to bishop by dint of sheer intellectual might. And, though comparatively settled now at the age of sixty-nine, he had narrowly escaped being defrocked the previous spring after an incident involving a goat, a gardener and a mother superior at a nunnery in Ballygoeasy. The Irish Catholic had missed the scoop but the Daily Mail had managed to cover it at some length under the headline RIGHT RANDY REVEREND IN CONVENT ROMP. The Sun, not to be outdone, had rendered it thus: ROISTERS IN THE CLOISTERS. MOTHER MAGDALENE BLOWS WHISTLE ON BISHOP'S FOUL TACKLE. Doctor Oddie was in fact quite a well-known figure in Ireland for whatever about his recreational pursuits he was widely recognised as a leading authority on twentieth century Irish literature. And it was this along with his outgoing personality that usually guaranteed him an interested audience.

So there he was, striding grimly along the margins of Maynooth's pristine lawns, kicking up gravel like a bear broken loose on a bad morning. Stopping near the bicycle shed he turned and in a voice that rumbled like rolling thunder he addressed the slavering hackpack (This description does not include the Irish Catholic, which had lagged sheepishly some way behind the others).

- Gentlemen, you have heard what my ... ah ... colleagues have had to say....

At this point Ozzie indicated his fellow bishops standing in a huddle on the steps of the seminary watching him warily.

- and it saddens me to have to tell you that they are talking through their episcopal arses.

His audience laughed boorishly (with the exception of the Irish Catholic which now stood at a discreet distance, ashen-faced, ashamed and appalled).

- The truth is, continued Doctor Oddie, seemingly oblivious to the animal spirits around him, - that they have sat in judgement on a book they haven't read¬ — apart, that is, from a few thumb-smeared bits that some ecclesiastical tit has told them are lewd. And, like schoolboys the world over, they have obsessed about what consenting adults do in the privacy of their own and others' bedrooms. I am sorry to have to say this, but these reverend gentlemen are not so much a bench of judges as a collection of short planks.

- Can we take it you like the book then? tittered the Star.

- What! cried the bishop. - I certainly do not. The book is worse than pornographic. It is *misleading*. Apart from one passably written love scene it devotes the guts of six hundred pages to descriptions of people torturing their souls about all the sinful sex they're having and then going off to the bathroom to empty their bladders and bowels. In short, it reads as if it was written by some sex-starved saddo who hasn't had a good crap in fifty years.

- What about the title, my lord? asked the Irish Catholic primly amid howls of hysteria from his fellow hacks.
- *Chamber Noises?* Is it not rather crude?

- Not so much crude, said Ozzie, - as childish. The title is simply a juvenile rip-off of James Joyce's *Chamber Music*.

- Did you know, continued the Irish Catholic earnestly, - that the author of this work has nevertheless been compared to Joyce?

The bishop's eminent eyebrows bristled like angry beetles.

- If Joyce were alive today he wouldn't be found dead writing stuff like this, he boomed. – Corrigan is trapped in the past. The modern man is fixated on sex only because he can't get enough of it and the modern woman is fixated on it because she can't get enough of the right people to have it with.

- But, reasoned the Daily Mail, - has Corrigan not tapped into the zeitgeist?

- Zeitgeist? In what way? demanded the bishop.

- The golden calf of sex, explained the Mail, furrowing its forehead.

- Or the golden goose, sniffed the Irish Catholic.

- Piffle! bellowed Ozzie. - Sex is neither calf nor goose. Sex is a small whipped ice cream. Nothing more than a little poke. Nice at the time but all over before you know it. No, if this so-called writer wishes to deal with major subjects he should concentrate on the real scourges of the world. The terrible triplets for a start.

- Who are they, my lord? enquired the Irish Catholic gravely.

- Not who. What. Greed, wilful ignorance and a failure of the imagination. Look around you. Multinationals milking the poor for as far as the eye can see. And just look what England is doing to Ireland. Look what Ireland is doing to Ireland for heaven's sake. Look what the U.S. and Russia are doing to the world. My God, millions are dying of hunger and disease, millions more are crying out for deliverance from ruthless governments and what do our bishops do? They sit round a table in Maynooth dribbling about sex.

At this the listeners doubled up merrily again (apart from the Irish Catholic, that is, which had remained resolutely upright throughout, removed from the raucous ribaldry around it).

- Exactly my opinion, spluttered the Sun.

- And while you're on the subject, added the News of the World, wiping some spittles from its chin, - what about the place Mister Corrigan has chosen to live? Is it not scandalous?

- What place is that? enquired the bishop.

- Muff! bayed all the hacks bar one.

- Yes? And what about it? frowned Doctor Oddie.

231

- Surely you're aware, said the Sun, beaming broadly, - that muff is another word for a woman's private parts.

At this point the Daily Mail emitted a loud snigger which it quickly converted to a sneeze.

- I find that reference offensive, snapped Ozzie. - I know Muff. I have been there several times and always found it a most delightful spot.

He glared at the Sun. - Your comments are insulting and uncalled for. I remember you from Ballygoeasy, young man, and I fully intend to report you to Mister Murdoch.

- You'd obviously prefer a political novel, my lord, said the Irish Catholic, moving the interview along.

- Well, thundered the bishop, - better that than a badly written one that spends six hundred pages chronicling the biological adventures and misadventures of men and women that seem to spend half their lives shuttling between the bedroom and the bathroom. It's not as if these topics haven't already been dealt with. They have been and with artistic integrity by our two national treasures.

- Who are they? came the chortling chorus.

- James Joyce and Samuel Beckett of course. Joyce did sex and Beckett did the bladder and the bowels. As Seamus Heaney so neatly put it at his poetry evening last summer in The Hungry Hen: "Joyce is choice but Sam's the man". And if you doubt Heaney's word, get your hands on a copy of *Molloy*. Or watch *Waiting for Godot*. Nobody does it like Beckett. Urinating, flatulating, defecating. He does the lot.

A sudden expression of mild rapture briefly transfigured the bishop's face.

- Beckett, he said softly, eyes misting slightly, - is the only writer who regularly turns bowel movements into full-blown concertos. Yes, Heaney was right. Sam is the man.

Then, just as quickly, his features darkened again.

- But as for this... book, gentlemen, he growled, - this excrescence, this pallid puddle of piddle. It is nothing less than a diabolical debacle of diarrhoeal delirium. In short, it's about as intellectually engaging as an enema performed by a junior doctor on crack. I have nothing more to say. Thank you.

EXILES
(Act Two)

Sometimes a silver lining is not enough.

The miles from Dublin were the sweetest he'd ever driven. Behind him was his triumphant appearance on the Late Late Show and ahead was another night of love with Melanie. She'd have watched the whole thing on television and would be so proud of him, happy with the way he'd handled Gay Byrne's probing questions, delighted at how he'd dealt with the redneck priest in the audience. He swung into Burnfoot village and then took the quiet winding road that would bring him back to Muff.

You're calling my book obscene, Father. You want to know why? Because you've sex on the brain. And that's a very funny place to have it, if you don't mind my saying.

He smiled at the memory of the priest's sickly rigid face and the liberated laughter from the audience.

For hundreds of years the Irish clergy have found sex a very handy stick to beat the faithful into submission with. But mark my words, Father, that stick may turn into a boomerang some day and come right back and hit you when you're least expecting it.

That was the coup de grâce. The poor man couldn't take any more and left the studio to a chorus of whistles and jeers.

A full bright moon flooded the night and lighted the road in front of him. He tingled with joy and felt so much at one with so many people that he would have been hard put to number them. A tenderness of regret came at him out of his elation as he suddenly thought of Conn and the friendship they'd once had. If only he could talk to him again, banter and share with him again, especially now at this perfect time. There was something about the affinity they'd had that wasn't quite there with Melanie. Strange, he thought, how sexual intensity colours so much and makes complete communication impossible. I could do with Conn now, he thought wistfully, a chastened, wiser Conn of course, one that doesn't crow about his conquests, one that doesn't covet Melanie. He rounded the last bend before Muff and stopped at the T junction that was almost opposite his home. To hell with ifs and buts, he thought. The way I feel now, any Conn would nearly do.

He pulled into the driveway at *Dedalus* at twenty minutes past three. When he switched off the engine he felt his shoulders loosen a little and he gave a long slow sigh, thinking of the pleasures that lay ahead. She'll be asleep now, he thought, dreaming of me and of the excitement of our life together. I'll stand looking at her awhile and wonder again at this miracle that is mine. Then I'll slip quietly into bed and hold her and kiss and caress her till she's roused. And she'll smile and kiss me back and touch me and make me ready.

He closed the front door and immediately a warning sound beat in his head. He stopped breathing for some seconds and listened. There were voices, two of them, hushed and confidential, and they were coming from the kitchen. Slowly, quietly, he took off his overcoat and hung it on the coat-stand and then, in a moment of clarity, he knew who was there and why. In spite of this he began to hum a little tune to himself, making it up as he went along (as he sometimes did in times of stress), wanting to believe that if he behaved normally then everything else would be normal in turn. Suddenly the kitchen door opened and Melanie stood framed in an oblong of light. White-haired and lovely-limbed she stood and a flame seemed to tremble on her face.

- Fuck away off, she said quietly.
- What! he gasped. - What did you just say?

She wore a pale lilac dressing gown which hung open all the way down, revealing the see-through slip he'd given her for their first night at *Dedalus*. She shook her long powder-white hair in shuddering contempt and Myles felt his loins leap with the thrill of her.

- Fuck you, you steaming heap of shite, she whispered.
- What's wrong? he cried. - What's the matter with you?

She moved forward a step, the full frontal beauty of her form gleaming through the slight slip.

- Scummy big bastard, she continued and somehow, despite the virulence of her views, her voice was as gentle as the dew of night, softer than the softest petal from a

237

windblown rose.

Myles stared in disbelief.

- What have I done? he shouted. - Tell me what I've done!

The tip of her tongue moistened her full red lips and her eyes flashed green fire. But then quickly, unexpectedly, her manner changed as she turned to speak to the other person in the kitchen.

- Come on, she coaxed, with a playful pout of her lovely mouth. - Yes, come on over. I want you to meet an old friend of yours.

The tall handsome figure of Conn came into view.

- Hello, Myles, he said. - Long time.

Myles was, as they say, shocked but not surprised. He was not surprised because he'd known who was there. He was shocked, however, for two reasons. Firstly, Conn looked years younger than he should have looked and also, his fly was wide open.

- It's good to see you, Conn, he croaked, trying to avert his eyes from the shadowy pink flesh that leered out at him, - but is it not a bit late to be callin?

- You're right, came the reply. - It is rather late. I should have been here nine years ago.

As Conn said this he became aware that Myles was goggling in horror at his gaping crotch. Whereupon he glanced unselfconsciously down, lowered his hands and brought up the zip with a satisfied *brrrp!*

- Is it *that* long? gasped Myles. - Is it really *that* long?

Melanie smiled and Myles felt as if his stomach had just been scooped hollow. He clutched at the coat-stand, leaning

238

on it so hard that it began to wobble and for a short time he and it seemed to cling to each other for support.

- Imagine! he gulped. - I can hardly believe it. Where have you been hidin yourself anyway?

- I haven't been hidin myself anywhere, said Conn calmly. - In fact, I haven't *been*.

- Oh really? squeaked Myles. His mind had temporarily emptied but the words kept coming. - That must be strange. To not even be.

In the course of this exchange between the two old friends Melanie had become quite restless and now she took a further step in Myles' direction, her kneecaps glinting ominously.

- You want to know what you are? she said to him, the pale sculpted beauty of her cheeks hued with a faint flush.

- What? he enquired pessimistically.

- You're a self-centred arsehole, that's what you are, she rasped.

- What the hell's goin on? spluttered Myles, taking a precautionary half pace backwards. - What's come over you?

- She's right, said Conn, reasonably. - It was bad enough the times you were drunk and you thought you were James Joyce. But now you're sober and you think you're God Almighty. It's ridiculous.

- That's not true! shouted Myles.

- Have you forgotten? said Conn. - I was your best friend, probably your only friend, and what did you do? You turned me into a sadist and a sodomite. *And* a paedophile. And as if that wasn't bad enough you then went and airbrushed me out of your life. Just so you could have Melanie all to yourself.

How's that for loyalty!

- I had to do it! cried Myles.

- You didn't *have* to do *any*thing, countered Conn.
- Nobody *has* to do *any*thing.

- I had to do it for the plot, quavered Myles. - The plot
wasn't goin anywhere. You should have heard Colm Herron
about it. He cracked up over it. Did you know that?

- And you took my red hair away! wailed Melanie. - My
lovely red hair!

- It didn't suit you, shouted Myles.

- It didn't suit *you*, she retorted. - And you know why?
Because you've no taste, that's why. Not a clue. Jesus.

- It's beautiful, insisted Myles.

- I *hate* white hair, she hissed. - It makes me look about
sixty.

She took another step towards him and she was so close
now that he could almost feel the heat of her breath on his
face.

- Oh, and another thing, she added.

- What?

- You've been fucking me under false pretences.

- What!

At this critical point the writer in him stirred uneasily.
*Surely she didn't need the word false there? After all, pretences
are pretences.*

- Twice a day for nine years!

- What do you mean, *false* pretences?

- I didn't tell you, she said, smiling bitterly. - Conn's been
showing me how to use the computer.

240

- Oh?

- Yes, she continued, - and we've been talking to another old friend of yours.

- Who's that?

- James.

- James ... James, he said slowly, frowning and shaking his head. - What James is that now?

- James Joyce. Remember him? she cried. - The one that wrote your book, you scheming shitehawk.

- He didn't write my book!

- And, by the way, interjected Conn, - he was delighted to hear how well it's doin in China....

- Oh good.

- but not so pleased to hear whose name's on it. He's kickin up hell about it. And he says he hopes he'll be seein you soon.

- Cheat! spat Melanie.

Conn came close behind her and put his arms around her front, pulling her tightly against him.

- Come on, love, he said. - He's not worth gettin worked up over.

Melanie's expression immediately transformed and she smiled adoringly up over her shoulder at Conn, wiggling her bum provocatively.

- Am *I*? she cooed.

The sight of them locked together, Conn's body where his should be, filled Myles with sudden outrage. At that moment he wanted this character gone, obliterated. But even as the thought dangled in his head he cut it loose and let it go. *Be careful what you wish for. Talk, don't wish. Where were we?*

- What's wrong with Joyce anyway? he demanded. - How can he be so petty, a man of his intelligence? The book's out there, being read by millions. What more does he want?

- And there was me thinking I was living with a fucking genius, sighed Melanie.

- I *am* a genius, declared Myles. - I knocked seven thousand pages down to six hundred. I had to plough through three million words nobody else would have read in a fit. *That's* genius.

- No, said Conn. - That's what a literary editor does.

- Hah! scoffed Myles. - Literary editors don't spend four years listenin to dead men dictatin words of sixteen syllables that aren't even words. The bastard nearly had me in Gransha so he did.

Melanie rushed forward with a sudden cry and Myles immediately cupped his hands defensively in front of him. But she dashed past him and went straight to the hall mirror.

- Look at me! she sobbed. - Look at that hair!

- What about your hair? retorted Myles, moving a little awkwardly in her direction on account of keeping himself protected. - It's lovely! I've never seen you lookin as well!

- Don't listen to him! shouted Conn. - It's terrible!

- She loved it! persisted Myles. - She always told me how much she loved it!

Melanie turned from the mirror to glare at Myles and then padded slowly towards him.

- What was that you just said? she whispered.

- You loved it, he whimpered. - You told me so.

- *You* made me say things. You made me *do* things. I was your raggedy doll, you dirty bastard.

Now when a man drives a car for three and a half hours without a break (as Myles had recently done) important changes can often take place in his undercarriage (as happened on this occasion with Myles). Add to that an encounter immediately afterwards with a sexually vigorous, very voluptuous, very nearly naked girl and, no matter how aggressively she behaves towards that man (in this instance, Myles), you have what is commonly referred to in sex therapy manuals as a case of the male member blindly believing it can stand up against a fury worse than hell.

So let's be done with it. She was almost on top of him now, a wild angel, a thing of unutterable beauty. She gave him a quiet haunting look and taking his willing hands and kneading them softly in hers she raised a dimpled knee and with crushing force slammed it into his goolies.

- Conn, she said, - take me to bed.

GRACE

There but for the grace of God go I.

A knee in the nuts is no fun in anybody's book but a broken heart is another story altogether. For even after the sensation of having been debollocksed by means of a series of dropped breeze blocks had faded to the merest tingle Myles' tears continued to fall. Through the rest of the night and into the morning they fell as he listened mortified to the startled gasps and delirious groans emanating from the spare bedroom.

At eight o'clock they left the creaking divan and repaired to the kitchen where the sounds of gentle domesticity did little to ease Myles' misery and shame: the popping toast, the clinking delph, the steaming kettle, the chatter from Melanie about the problems of getting a good plumber to come back a second time. This respite (such as it was) proved short-lived however. Within ten minutes a saucepan was knocked into the sink during what was clearly an unequal struggle and they were immediately at it again, first on the breakfast table, then on the floor. Above the drumming of her heels on the non-slip tiles he heard her complain that she'd only had a half a cup of tea and two bites of toast but very soon her complaints turned to moans of delight and a stream of unsavoury suggestions as to what Conn might do next.

After what seemed to Myles like a very long time the moans quietened to sighs and slowly to silence and he lay in the bed, his life over. And, without knowing why, he found that his eyes were being drawn as if by compulsion to certain small features around him: the milky light that stole in and touched the cornice above the closed curtains, the hairline crack like a Z on the ceiling just to his left of the chandelier, the place where two strips of wallpaper had never quite met. In a half dream he wondered why he was hanging so stubbornly on these silly little things that he'd looked at without thinking for nine years. And then he remembered something he'd once read about how grief can derange the mind, how bereaved people go through waves of believing that all that's needed to bring their loved one back is to be alone with the familiar. It might be a footstep on the stairs or perhaps the click of a door somewhere that lets them know the moment has arrived. But whatever it is, when it happens they will look up and the person will be there, smiling.

So when the bedroom door opened and Melanie came in, her eyes shining, he knew. And when she lay beside him and asked him to warm her up he did what she wanted. And while he held her tightly she told him about the letter the postman had brought.

- It's from the surgery, she said. - I'm pregnant.

So he kissed her and she whispered - Why are you crying? You told me you wanted a baby.

- I do, he said. - I've never been as happy in my life.

His tears came faster now and she dabbed at them with her soft white hair.

- Then why are you crying? she asked him.

- I had a nightmare, he told her, - just as I woke up. It was terrible.

- Poor pet. What was it?

- I can't remember, he said. - It was so bad I nearly wanted to die but I can't remember.

- That happens me sometimes, she said, kissing his pale wet cheeks. - Dreams are funny things.

AFTERWORD

My dear reader,

If it's true that the winners write history (and it is) then it's also true that the right write novels. For the novelist is never wrong. Never. Never never never. Got it? Never.

Hold on. There *is* one exception and his name appears on the front cover of this book. No, not James Joyce. The other one. Yes. Colm Herron. Forget about him. The proper novelist is perfect in all things and for all time.

Now Conn was wrong when he accused Myles of thinking he was God Almighty. The truth is that Myles didn't just think he was God Almighty. He was. That is, I am. Or, put another way,

IAMWHOAM!

It's all to do with creating something out of nothing, you see, and making you believe what I want you to believe. That Conn, for example, will one day return to claim back his life and his love. (Dream on, dummy). Or that Myles will eventually be found out and get his comeuppance. (Forget it, mutt. It's not going to happen). Or that, in order to satisfy the ravings of a washed-up fucked-up locked-up loony, it's okay to end a novel with the word and.